AETURNUM

THE BOOK OF ADAM
BOOK TWO

SCOTT GELOWITZ

For Jennifer,
Jessica, Zachary, Rachel, and Rebecca.

Thank you for putting up with me and my hobby.

CONTENTS

ACKNOWLEDGEMENTS

Thank you to my Family and Beta Reader team:

Charles and Anne Gelowitz,
Cherie Frick,
Luke Frick,
Jennifer Gelowitz,
Kim Schaan,
and Kim Merasty.

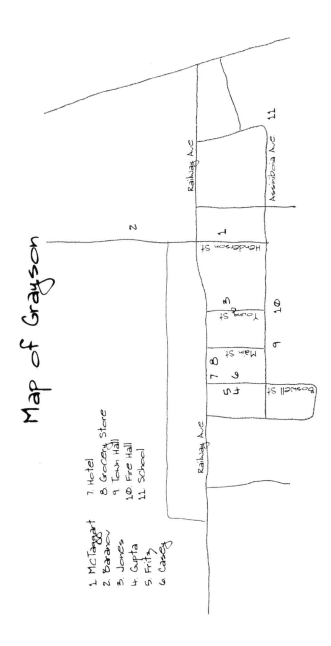

Map of Grayson

1. McTaggart
2. Barakov
3. Jones
4. Gupta
5. Fritz
6. Casey

7. Hotel
8. Grocery Store
9. Town Hall
10. Fire Hall
11. School

Railway Ave

Henderson St

Young St

Main St

Boswell St

Railway Ave

Assiniboia Ave

CHAPTER ONE

Adam sat in the chair feeling uncomfortable.

It wasn't that the chair was uncomfortable. The chair was perfectly fine. It was what he had just been told.

"We don't know many details yet, but they nearly had him at the prison when it happened."

Gurpreet Gupta looked at Adam as he spoke in his low voice and rich East-Indian accent. Concern showed in his eyes, although the rest of him seemed calm.

Adam had just been informed that Larix had escaped. Aggie's warning had been correct, even down to the time of day. The realization gave Adam goose bumps as Aggie's words triggered a flood of memories while the others in the room continued discussing the news.

Adam remembered the day Kevin burst into his garage to tell him that the residents of Waldron had disappeared and the town was in shambles. A mysterious fog surrounded Waldron and when it cleared no one could be found. The same thing had happened a week before at another town, Langenburg.

That news came right after Adam had discovered his dad's mysterious lapel pin. At that point he had no idea how significant that discovery would be.

He also remembered listening to Don Chen and Gurpreet Gupta telling him and his friends about the Sentinel League – the centuries old secret organization that built the town. Most surprising was the fact that almost all of the adults in town were members.

A lot of information was shared in that short meeting, like the revelation that the stories of Atlantis were mostly true but the inhabitants of the island, called the Teneo and Decreta, had one major disagreement between them – how to treat the 'Common' people living everywhere else in the world. The Teneo believed that Mankind were capable of evolving and learning – one day to be as intelligent as they. The Decreta believed that Mankind would never be anything more than mildly intelligent so they should be used as lab rats to further their own scientific knowledge.

Suddenly, Elianora's face popped up in his mind. It was the first time he had ever seen Elianora and soon after Grayson had been surrounded by the fog. He immediately recognized her from the picture of people standing in front of Town Hall at the Grand Opening in 1910. She looked so young but yet she was really old. Just how old he didn't know, but he knew it was centuries.

Elianora had shown the boys the history of Larix, the leader of the Decreta, and the power he controlled in the Heartstone - the mysterious glowing object he carried with him always – using it to control Mankind and kill anyone, including the Teneo, who stood in his way. No Teneo could get near without causing it to explode, but 'Common' humans could. In 1908 at the battle of Tunguska, Larix had lost the Heartstone and believed it destroyed, but it was found by one of the Sentinel League members soon after. Since then it had been guarded by the Sentinel League under the supervision of Elianora, moved from hiding place to hiding place and eventually ending up in the small town of Grayson – a tiny town in the middle of nowhere in Canada - and there it stayed for far too long.

Tasked with helping to keep the Heartstone hidden, Adam thought about how lucky he and his friends had been to escape being caught time and again. They found the Keystone in Town Hall and arrived back to Elianora just in time to see her shot full of the drug that was controlling the townspeople, making them tell their most intimate secrets while acting like zombies. The sound of the gunshot in his memory still made Adam jump.

Elianora had believed that no drug could control her - but she was wrong. She told Larix exactly where the boys were hiding and that they also had the Keystone.

The group split up in order to keep the Keystone from Larix and hopefully save all of the townspeople. Adam decided that he and Kevin would try to find the Heartstone and get it out of town, but they needed to get to the site where it was hidden first. Although he would have liked to forget it, the memory of riding double with Kevin on Elianora's flowery bicycle crept into his mind.

It was the only way, he reminded himself often.

The flood of memories continued as Adam remembered hearing his mother's voice while climbing out of the caves hidden under the Radome - the huge golf ball shaped structure located south of town. Her voice lured him out to be caught by Larix, who had already drugged Kevin a couple of minutes earlier.

Larix explained to Adam that the Keystone was actually called an Impression Stone, an object that can store instructions within forever. The Impression Stone would have instructions how to navigate the Radome caves and get past the traps, but only Adam had the ability to connect with it and receive those instructions. Larix promised that if Adam helped, Larix would leave Grayson without hurting anyone. Not believing him, Adam led Larix and two of his soldiers through the caves anyway since he had no other choice.

The rest was a blur as Adam made it through the traps and finally to the last chamber where he pulled the Heartstone from its hiding spot. Only, it wasn't really the Heartstone – just a fake. He connected with it and read the instructions inside:

"To whoever is connected with this stone: this is not the Heartstone you are looking for. It is a copy. The real Heartstone has been taken away without the knowledge of Elianora or any others in the Sentinel League, in the hopes of keeping it safe.

We know our locations have been compromised. Elianora was unwilling to believe, so we have taken over."

A strange symbol appeared at the end of the message.

It was at that moment that he decided he would have to run for it and hope for some luck. He didn't run *as if* his life depended on it; he ran *because* his life depended on it.

At the end of his run fueled by fear fear, he sprinted up the last steps leading out of the caves and dove to the side quickly.

That's when he heard the two gunshots.

At that moment he thought he was dead, but instead of drifting in to darkness, he heard the gruff voice of Ben Casey. It was far from angelic, but it sounded like safety to Adam.

The last wave of memory was the warning from Aggie as he sat in front of the grocery store, one week after the events in the Radome caves. "Larix is about to escape," was the last thing he remembered Aggie saying before he was pulled back to reality once more.

Don Chen paced in front of the crackling fireplace in Elianora's living room. "I don't get it. It *had* to be an inside job, but we hand-selected the transport team ourselves. They were top military people." He banged his hand on the mantle in frustration.

Elianora sat silently in her rocking chair, knitting a pink pastel blanket while she listened. The firelight reflected on her face since it was the only source of light in the room that evening. The Lumiens on the ceiling above were left sleeping and cast no light. The Lumiens, Adam had discovered, were microscopic creatures that consumed carbon dioxide and released light when they were awake. They were one of the many secrets the Sentinel League protected.

Don's frustrated strike brought Elianora out of her silence.

"Don't be too hard on yourselves. You know as well as I do that this isn't the first time he's escaped – and we've thought we covered all of the loopholes each of the other times too."

Don shrugged in a reluctant agreement. "I know, but it's just so *frustrating*. We thought we could let down our guard for a while."

Elianora nodded. "His history tells us that we *can* relax - for a while," she replied. "Larix usually hides for some time before he starts poking around again. We've rattled his cage and he doesn't feel quite as invincible as he did before."

"On another note," said Gurpreet, "So far it's only the senior members of the League that know exactly what happened in the Radome caves, if you don't count the four boys. Have we decided to let the boys keep those memories?"

"I've given it a lot of thought," said Elianora, "and I think we will let things stay as they are, but we must impress upon the boys the importance of the secrecy of the message inside. It seems that a lot of people in the Sentinel League already know about the Heartstone."

Gurpreet nodded. "It would have been too risky to wipe the memories of all our townspeople, plus the ones in Waldron and Langenburg. Especially the children."

"Maybe it's for the best," said Elianora.

Adam sat and listened, but up to that point he had felt as though he were eavesdropping rather than having been invited in on the conversation.

Elianora turned to Adam. "You've told Gurpreet about your encounter with Aggie, but can you tell me *exactly* what she said?"

Adam pushed his memory, trying to make sure he got it right. It *had* just happened a few hours before, but he wanted to be as accurate as possible.

"She said, 'Larix is about to escape. He thinks it was your fault he was captured and that you know where the real Heartstone is. He *will* come for you, but I can't see when. You need to stay safe.' Then she shivered and continued on with Martha like nothing had happened."

Elianora nodded, absorbing the words as Adam spoke. Adam waited for her to say something until he couldn't hold back the question that had been bothering him almost as much as the fact that Larix had escaped.

"How did Aggie know that he was going to escape? Is she some kind of psychic?"

Elianora and Gurpreet exchanged looks, and after a pause Elianora nodded.

"Well," said Gurpreet. "Kind-of. She is a special type of psychic – one that doesn't realize what she's said afterward. We call her an 'inter'. It's short for 'intermediate'. There are lots of names for what she does, though, like medium or seer. It's a pretty rare gift, but it doesn't work like you see in the movies. When she gets a signal or message, she understands it completely in the moment but always loses it afterward. Sometimes she thinks she's in the future moment that she is talking about, and other times she knows it's the present and she's telling about the future, like when she told you about Larix coming back. It happened more when she was younger, but now that she's older it rarely happens. We actually thought she was done intermediating big events anymore. When it happens now she mostly just tells everyone what the person next to her will have for lunch the next day."

A thought came to Adam about a story Mark had told him.

"You never told Aggie about your anniversary present when she spilled the beans to your wife, did you?" asked Adam.

Gurpreet shook his head. "Nope. She got a signal in the checkout line at the store because my wife was next to her. Too bad Mark was there at the time."

"So she doesn't remember anything she says?" asked Adam.

Gurpreet shook his head. "We've told her about it over the years, but she doesn't really believe us."

Adam nodded, although he didn't totally understand. "Doesn't Martha realize what Aggie is doing? She was there each time Aggie said something about the future but she didn't seem to think it was strange."

"It's hard to explain, but Aggie and Martha are a lot the same. Martha is like an antenna for Aggie and Aggie gets more signals with her around. Martha has the same lack of memory as Aggie afterward," said Gurpreet.

"Those two have an interesting history, but we will leave that for some other time," said Elianora. "Right now, it's getting late and you should be getting home." She looked at Don and Gurpreet who nodded back.

She looked to Adam. "Thank you for coming out here and telling me what you know." She grabbed his hand. "I wanted you to be the first to hear about the escape because of your involvement, and I was worried how you might react. Now, I want you to relax and not worry about Larix at all. Aggie has been wrong in the past, and she told you she couldn't see when Larix might come back. That tells me that it is far enough in the future to be out of her sight, ok?"

Adam nodded as she patted his hand. Her words relaxed the knot in his gut somewhat, but not completely.

The concern she showed him felt so foreign. Until recently, his own mother had never shown much concern for him – at least as far as he could remember. Elianora should have felt like a grandmother to Adam, but because he had never met his grandparents he didn't know what that would feel like either.

"If you get upset or start to feel afraid," she put her hand up to stop any response, "I know - you're thirteen and won't admit it if you're afraid anyway, but, if you do start to feel funny please come and see me anytime. We've decided to let you keep your Dad's lapel pin so you can take the tunnels out here whenever you need. Just don't tell everyone we let you keep it, alright?"

Adam nodded. He was happy that they let him keep the pin, as it was the biggest connection he had to his father.

"Let's get you home," said Don, motioning for the door.

Adam pulled his hand away from Elianora, although he didn't want to. Just her contact made him feel safer.

"Thanks for telling me, and thanks for letting me keep the pin. It means a lot," said Adam.

Elianora nodded and smiled. She understood.

"We'll talk tomorrow after I get some reports," Gurpreet said to Elianora.

"You know where to find me," she replied. "And you two need to relax as well." She pointed at Gurpreet and Don. "We're in a better position now than we were just a few weeks ago because we know Larix is in hiding again. We can analyze what happened over the next couple of months, but it does no good if everyone is stressed out and not sleeping." She gave them a look like a mother scolding her children.

Adam found it amusing that the two men looked like little boys being given a lecture by a parent.

"Yes ma'am," replied Gurpreet as Don opened the door and led the way outside.

The night was clear and calm. An owl hooted in the hills nearby while the crickets chirped. It was a beautiful night in mid-summer as they walked toward the tunnel. They would return the same way they came – via the school. Adam had asked why they went that way, when the 6:00 tunnel went directly to Elianora's. The way through the school was a little extra distance.

The men chuckled and Don replied, "We aren't thirteen anymore. Walking the extra distance is easier than getting on our hands and knees and crawling through that crawlspace. Besides, my wife would be upset with the dirt on my pants and worn out knees."

Gurpreet nodded in agreement.

Adam hadn't thought about it that way, but since they had pointed it out to him he couldn't help but think that it was going to suck to get old.

CHAPTER TWO

Summer slipped away and school started once again. Life in Grayson had returned to normal fast, as if nothing unusual had happened that summer. News of the Sentinel League became old, and soon the standard motion of the town took over. Someone observant enough could set their watch by the daily movements of most of the residents.

One of the few changes to happen was the addition of another class in school – History of the Sentinel League, taught by Ms. Howey. She was young, as far as teachers go, and had moved back to Grayson after recently finishing her own schooling. Because it was her first year teaching and this was the first time the Sentinel League history was being taught to school kids, the class was boring and seemed quite pointless. Adam tried to listen and learn as much as he could, but it was hard to hear over the multiple conversations going on at the same time during the class. Ms. Howey was far from strict.

By far the biggest change was the interest in League Kurling. It began almost as a side note when teaching the older initiates about the Sentinel League. After a quick field trip to watch Karl Klein give a demonstration, the townspeople asked to see a full game. The following Sunday afternoon, Marius Miller and Karl played against each other, giving instruction throughout. The field was so packed with spectators that during the next week bleachers were built so everyone could see the game. Soon everyone wanted to try this new sport, but there were few people who could make even the smallest connection with the stones. Coincidentally, more windows were broken by adults in the following month than had been broken by children in the many years prior.

Because of his knack for the game, Adam enjoyed learning everything he could about Kurling and practiced any chance he could. He still had a hard time believing that he was actually able to alter the flight path of an ordinary stone as it flew though the air. It seemed like something out of a wild fantasy novel. The fact that his father had also excelled at the game helped fuel his passion.

When Karl Klein offered to give him some extra training in the early spring, Adam jumped at the chance. Every few days after the snow melted they would find some time to play a game against each other. Karl taught Adam new throws and strategy (usually by using them to beat Adam) and Adam got better at it every time, sometimes even getting close to winning.

At home, Adam and his mother slipped back into their old routine. He tiptoed around Mary and she grunted whenever she heard him. The only surprise was on his Fourteenth birthday when Mary brought home a chocolate cake and actually put candles on it for him to blow out. It was a frozen cake from the store, not a homemade one like Kevin usually had, but it tasted fantastic.

Adam almost forgot about the events of the previous summer too. One Saturday he woke up from a nightmare about Larix returning so he decided to visit Elianora. Mrs. Jones was working that Saturday and let him use the file room entrance to the tunnels, but he didn't have to ask. They had let him keep his key to Town Hall as well as the lapel pin.

He didn't mind using the 6:00 tunnel that led directly to Elianora's. Even though his pants *did* get a little dirty crawling through the crawlspace, he washed his own laundry anyway.

Once he arrived, Elianora put him at ease by assuring him that the League had heard nothing unusual, and it would be a long time yet before Larix would come out of hiding.

In this way, the months passed by, and soon summer came again.

Adam knocked on the side door.

A moment later it opened. Kevin was chewing something as he nodded at Adam, obviously having expected him.

"Sorry, did I interrupt you while you were eating?" Adam asked. Adam knew the Baranov's usually ate as a family, so he didn't want to interrupt. "I can come back," he continued.

Kevin shook his head as he swallowed hard. "Nope, you don't have to. We were done eating half an hour ago."

Adam gave Kevin a confused look, and Kevin knew Adam well enough to understand the unspoken question.

"I saw you coming up the driveway and I grabbed a snack on the way to answer the door."

"I guess you could call it your 'second supper'." Adam chuckled.

Kevin's eyes widened. "Was that a 'Lord of the Rings' reference? Really?"

Adam laughed while Kevin palmed his forehead.

"It's bad enough that Mark is always quoting 'The Lord of the Rings', but I didn't expect that kind of thing from you," Kevin smiled as he put his hand down, showing that he *did* find it a little funny.

"So, what's the plan for tonight?" asked Adam.

"I dunno," Kevin replied. "We could go to the school and watch the men play ball. Maybe some of the guys will be there."

Adam nodded. "If we get bored we can always practice throwing some stones. Maybe have a little Kurling game."

"Yep – that sounds good. Let me grab my shoes and we'll go."

Adam waited as Kevin went back in the house. It was the beginning of July and the evenings had finally been nice. The previous winter had been one of the coldest on record with the most snow in the last 50 years, and the last traces of water had only disappeared a week prior. The recent warm days were a welcome relief, lending to a good turnout at the ball games.

Kevin stepped outside and breathed the fresh air deeply. He walked over to the shed and pulled out his bike, closing the door behind him. Adam glided next to him on his own bike, and soon they were pedaling out the long driveway, as they had done many times before.

"Are your mom and sisters coming to the game?" asked Adam.

Kevin nodded. "They all left with Dad right after we ate. I stayed to wait for you and do the dishes."

After a short ride they arrived at the ball diamonds next to the school. The adult men's team was playing against the team from Killaly and it seemed like most of both towns were there to watch. Adam had learned that Killaly was another Sentinel League town but they had a lot less residents that were members. That meant that the boys wouldn't be able to practice their Kurling throws while the other team was in town.

They stood their bikes in the rack near the school and walked to the fence beside first base, since that was the nearest open spot. Kevin's dad Mikhail Baranov, or Mike to his friends, was pitching to the other team. Marius Miller was on first base and nodded to the boys when he noticed them walking up then returned his attention to the game.

Mike threw the first pitch and it was a strike. The second one was a strike again. He wasn't so lucky with the third one, though, and the batter connected hard with the ball, driving it right toward Adam's face.

Adam jerked his head backwards and felt the ball brush past his nose. It missed by the width of a hair. He quickly put his hand to his face as a reaction to the shock. The crowd gasped when they saw his movements, but relaxed when he took his hand from his face and gave everyone a thumbs-up to say he was ok.

"Maybe we should go find another spot to watch," said Kevin.

Adam nodded and they stepped away from the fence. As they started looking for another spot, Mark popped out of the crowd, waving to his friends.

Kevin looked at Mark, then turned and ran a couple of steps in the opposite direction. Adam stopped as Kevin turned back again, laughing at his actions. Since the events of the previous summer, Kevin and Mark had become better friends - although you couldn't tell it from the way they usually acted, teasing each other at every opportunity.

Mark was munching on some type of bagged treat as he approached. "I thought you guys would show up sometime," he said through the crumbs in his mouth. "You wanna watch the game or go do something else?" he asked.

"I was hoping to watch," said Adam, "but there aren't any better spots to watch from than where we were."

"We could go further out from where you were. The view would be worse, but it would be a lot safer," said Mark.

Adam considered it for a moment, then remembered his recent scare and agreed.

Kevin added, "And if we don't like it, we can just find another spot."

The three walked down the fence line until it ended and then continued for another fifty feet. There they reached a large tree. It stood where the fence line would have gone if it had continued. The tree was just large enough that all three could lean against it and still be facing the game, more or less.

After watching the inning change so that the Killaly team was now in the field, Adam began scanning the crowd. There was a good mix of Grayson and Killaly people in the bleachers, and he recognized some of the visitors from events over the years.

He spotted Jimmy sitting near the top next to Trevor and Kassie, who were snuggled close together. Jimmy was clearly making an effort not to notice them as they exchanged affectionate movements. It had been nearly a year since the two started dating, so Kevin was no longer over-protective of his sister. Both Kevin and Jimmy felt the same way about the couple's public displays of affection, though, and would fake throwing up if they were in the vicinity.

Face by face Adam looked through the crowd, until he saw one that looked out of place. Even at that distance he knew who it was.

Elianora.

It was shocking since he had never seen her in town before, let alone sitting among the people at a community event. She glanced in his direction and nodded, giving him a friendly smile, and he did the same in return.

A loud crack sounded in the air as Karl Klein connected with the last pitch. It was a solid hit, straight up the first baseline toward the boys, but still in play. The Killaly outfielder grabbed the ball before it reached the boys and whipped it to the first baseman. Karl had just made it to first in time, although he looked as if it took all the effort he had. His face was such a bright red that Adam was worried that Karl wasn't getting any air, but after a few great puffs his color began returning to normal again.

The last play had taken Adam's attention away from Elianora. When he looked back to see her again, she was gone. *Why would she leave before the first inning is done?* he wondered.

In a matter of seconds his thoughts were back on the game. Mark cheered when his father, Gurpreet, came up to bat. Gurpreet was an excellent ball player, whereas his son Mark was terrible at the sport. Gurpreet stood still, waiting intently for the pitch. The first one was a ball, way too high. The second one was perfect, and Gurpreet took full advantage. He hit the ball far down the middle of the field and took off running for first.

Karl moved his massive frame as fast as he could, which was a lot faster than the boys expected, but by the time he was passing third base Gurpreet was nearly behind him. Halfway to home plate, Gurpreet had to slow down because he couldn't pass Karl.

The ball had made it back to second base and was about to be thrown home as they neared. It was going to be close. Gurpreet turned back to third base, realizing both he and Karl wouldn't make it home before the ball. Karl dove and slid for the plate as the ball screamed toward home. Luckily for Karl, the throw from second base had gone high while he had gone low. He slid just far enough that his first two fingers touched the plate. The umpire called him safe.

The crowd clapped and cheered for Karl as he rolled over and got to his feet uneasily. The boys weren't sure if the redness in his face was due to the running or everyone cheering for him. Even the back catcher for the Killaly team congratulated Karl on making it to home plate.

When the excitement died down, Karl brushed himself off as he walked over to the dugout.

As Adam watched Karl return and Mr. Garagan come up to bat, something caught his eye. Elianora was returning to her seat, but this time she wasn't alone.

"Guys!" said Adam, "Look."

He pointed to where Elianora sat.

"Is that who I think it is?" asked Mark.

"I don't believe it," said Kevin.

Sitting down next to Elianora was old George Fritz.

CHAPTER THREE

It had been almost a year since the boys had seen George. While he was gone no-one would tell them where George was so they had quit asking. Eventually they forgot to ask anymore.

George looked completely different. He was clean-shaven, his clothes were neat, and his hair didn't look like he had just rolled out of bed. The stark difference between the old George and the new George made Adam wonder what exactly he had been through, although Adam wasn't sure he wanted to know.

The game ended up being a nail biter, with the Grayson men winning by one run. The two teams shook hands and many of the players obviously knew each other well by the comments between them.

The boys watched various people walking past George, shaking his hand and saying a few words before moving on. They guessed that a lot of the comments were, 'You're looking good' and 'Good to see you."

"Do we go say hi?" asked Kevin, not sounding totally sure he wanted to. Even though George looked better than he had previously, the memory of him still seemed to rub Kevin the wrong way.

Adam nodded.

"Come on you big baby," said Mark who started walking toward George as the other two followed.

As they got closer the crowd thinned out. George and Elianora stood to leave.

"Hi George," said Mark, "It's good to see you again."

George smiled. "Hello Mark – hello boys. Good to see you too." He looked as if he were straining to keep a smile on his face.

"I was hoping you three would come over and talk to us," said Elianora, taking over the conversation. "We need to recruit you for a job tomorrow, ok? It's a League job and you *are* still technically initiates."

Adam looked at the other two and nodded for the group. "What do you need?" he asked.

"We would like you to come over to George's after lunch. He needs some help organizing things now that he's back home again. I've already spoken to Jimmy about helping out too," said Elianora.

"We'll be there," said Kevin with a smile.

Adam knew Kevin was putting up a brave front.

"Good," said Elianora. "We need to get George settled yet tonight so we'd better be going. See you tomorrow."

George nodded goodbye but didn't say another word.

"See you at 1 o'clock," said Mark as Elianora and George walked away.

As soon as they were far enough out of sight, Adam spoke.

"That was completely unexpected," he said.

"You're not kidding," said Kevin.

"He must have just gotten back today. There haven't been any lights on in his trailer since he left last year. Dad and I have been checking on the place while he was gone, but I didn't think he was ever coming back," said Mark.

"I heard that he went even crazier after Larix got to him," said Kevin. "But he looked better than I've ever seen him."

"He *looked* better, but something was off," added Adam.

"I thought that too," said Mark.

"Maybe he'll tell us something tomorrow," said Adam, "but let's not push it."

Mark and Kevin agreed.

"What should we do now?" asked Mark.

Adam shrugged and thought about it for a moment. "Do you have your bike here?" he asked Mark, "We brought ours."

Mark shook his head. "No, I came with Mom and my sisters. I told them not to wait for me when I saw you."

"Well, it's starting to get dark out so we can't practice Kurling," said Adam, Why don't we just go to my garage and play some cards for a while?"

"Sounds good to me," said Kevin.

Mark looked at Adam. "Well, since I don't have a bike maybe I can ride yours while you two ride together." Mark pointed at the pair. "I know Kevin's bike doesn't have any flowers like the bike you rode last year, but you guys shouldn't mind riding together again, right?"

Adam looked at Kevin who hung his head.

"I knew that would haunt me," said Kevin, although he had a small smile that he tried to hide.

Adam chuckled. "Fat chance. I'm more than willing to walk my bike home instead of doing that again. I swear my back still hurts from last year."

With that, the three walked toward Adam's garage.

The next day Kevin found Adam pulling apart some old piece of electronics in his garage. It was 12:30 and they would have to be at George's soon.

"Did you eat yet?" asked Kevin.

Adam set down his tools.

"Yep. Had some sort of canned stew that was leftover from last night. It was bad the first day, but at least it was worse the second." Adam laughed at his own sarcasm.

Kevin didn't laugh, feeling bad because he had just finished a large lunch with many choices of food.

"Should we go get Jimmy and then head over to George's?" asked Kevin.

"Sounds like a plan," answered Adam.

The two stepped outside and began walking toward Jimmy's.

"I am really dreading this," Kevin admitted on the way.

"I thought you would be," said Adam, "so I brought you these -"

Adam reached in his pocket and pulled out a pair of surgical rubber gloves, handing them to Kevin with a chuckle.

Kevin laughed at the gesture.

"That's not all," said Adam. He reached in his other pocket and pulled out two small pieces of foam.

"They're ear plugs. Once we get instructions, you won't have to listen to George OR Mark. Things should be pretty pleasant for you after that."

Kevin took the gloves and ear plugs, laughing the whole time.

They arrived at Jimmy's house just as Jimmy was walking down his driveway.

"Ladies," said Jimmy.

"M'am," said Adam with a nod.

They all smiled and said no more as they walked toward the Fire Hall.

As they reached the corner, a car raced past. It turned at Town Hall and parked around the back. They all recognized the car since it belonged to the Mayor, Jeff Wyndum.

Adam broke the silence. "I don't think I've ever seen Jeff in a hurry before, especially to get to work. I wonder what's up?"

Jimmy couldn't resist. "I'll bet he has a hot date and forgot his wallet at work. His dates get pretty expensive, you know. Like $12.99 a minute and long distance charges apply."

Adam and Kevin howled with laughter.

As they walked past Town Hall, Adam couldn't help but wonder why Jeff really was in a hurry. Jeff had seemed to take the news of the Sentinel League quite well when he had found out. Adam had expected him to be depressed at the fact that he wasn't invited to join previously, but it didn't take long before Jeff had come up with many reasons why. On top of that, he tried to make it sound like he had known about the Sentinel League all along – even telling Adam that he had known about the drawbridge doors in Town Hall and the Fire Hall since he was a boy.

Soon the group was nearing George's, and saw an old truck parked out front. Mark was flopped over the tailgate while Gurpreet and George talked. Mark looked like a young child waiting for their parent to finish a long conversation about accounting. As soon as he saw his friends approaching he perked up and tried to stand as if he were involved in the conversation.

Gurpreet faced the direction of the boys as he spoke to George. When he noticed the group approaching he motioned for George to look. George turned and his face broke into a wide smile.

"Hello boys," said George, waving them in as they neared.

George shook each boy's hand as they walked up. "Thank you, thank you. Thanks for helping a crazy old man." He seemed in a much better mood than the previous day.

Adam stole a glance at Kevin and Jimmy. "Uh...no problem," he managed to reply, "Glad we could help."

George looked like a puppy that had just seen its owner after a week away. The joy shone in his eyes like Adam had never seen before, but more that that, George looked *sane*. The constant look of suspicion was gone from his face, which made him look so different, as it had once been one of his most defining features. He had looked that way the entire time Adam had known him.

"We borrowed the town garbage truck and a bunch of garbage bags so that you could help George get rid of some of the 'information' that he collected over the years. Before you ask, you should know that George has been fully informed about the Sentinel League. He has very little memory of the time from when he became a member until just after he woke up from the accident that caused his memory loss. Since his run in with Larix his memory is slowly coming back, but don't bother him with a bunch of questions, ok?"

Adam threw a questioning glance at Kevin before nodding.

"So we're just here to help clean up?" asked Kevin.

Gurpreet nodded. "We need young muscle to carry bags and boxes out to the garbage truck. Since George knows about the Sentinel League again and most of the paperwork he collected was him trying to find out about the League, there's no point in keeping it anymore. George will go through the boxes to make sure there is nothing important inside and you will carry the garbage out to the truck. I have a few things to do at home, so when the truck is full come get me and I'll take it to the dump. Sounds good?"

The boys nodded.

"Great," said Gurpreet. He turned to George. "Let's get started. They'll follow you."

George nodded and walked to his door. One step in, he opened the first box and rifled though the contents. A minute later, he turned back to the group and handed out the first box.

"This one can go."

Adam was the closest one to the door, so he stepped in and grabbed the box. When he exited he wasn't surprised to see that Kevin was next in line. Jimmy was behind Kevin, and Mark stood far behind Jimmy, looking as though he would rather be anywhere else.

For the next hour they continued like ants taking food to the colony, although they were in reverse. Soon the truck was filled to the brim and Mark ran home to get his dad. When Gurpreet arrived, he took Jimmy and Mark along to the dump to unload, leaving Adam and Kevin behind since there were only three seats in the old truck.

"I can't thank you boys enough for all your help," said George, so happy that he seemed to choke up as he was talking.

"Don't thank us too much, Mr. Fritz. We owe you," said Adam.

Kevin looked at him and raised an eyebrow.

"Please, call me George...but I don't understand how you owe me anything?"

Kevin's raised eyebrow agreed with George.

"If it wasn't for your warnings, we wouldn't have ended up looking for answers and we would have ended up like Waldron and Langenburg."

George thought about it and nodded with a small smile. "You give me too much credit, Adam, but thank you."

Kevin nodded along with George, understanding Adam's logic.

"Anyway, we're getting pretty close to the end of my boxes. Before the others get back, how about we sit down and have a Root Beer? I put some in the fridge to cool this morning. It was a good thing Mark didn't know where I hid the last case or it would have been gone already."

Adam and Kevin laughed.

George motioned for them to sit at the table. Since taking all the boxes away, the kitchen table and chairs had been excavated. The boys were now able to sit in spots where they couldn't even see chairs before. The first time they had seen the table, they had been amazed at the amount of paper George had managed to successfully stack on top without the stacks toppling over.

George brought two cans from the fridge, handed one to each boy and sat in his usual chair. The seat where George had sat down was the only spot that had been clear of boxes before the cleaning, although there were still a few blank papers and some pencils in that spot on the table.

"You know, I used to enjoy drawing and sketching a lot – before I lost my memory, that is. Since I've been working with Elianora, I've started to do it again," said George. "It's quite relaxing."

"Do you have any of your drawings here?" asked Kevin.

Adam was surprised that Kevin would even ask, considering how Kevin felt about George. This new George must have been winning Kevin over.

George looked surprised too. "Yes, actually." He reached over to the kitchen counter nearby and grabbed a small stack of papers, handing one to Kevin.

Kevin looked at it with surprise. "This is *really* good," he exclaimed, handing it to Adam. The picture was a drawing of Town Hall.

"I did that completely by memory while I was...away." He seemed to feel awkward about saying the last word. After a second, he shook off the feeling and handed another picture over. It was a picture of the Hotel, once again really well done.

"You could sell these," said Kevin, quite serious.

"I don't know about that...you think so?" asked George, sheepish.

"For sure," said Kevin. "I'd bet my parents would buy one. Do you have any farm scenes? They love those."

George was surprised by Kevin's comments. His face broke into a wide smile.

"You know, I think there's a picture of a sunrise over the valley that I'm not quite done yet. Let me see," said George as he flipped through the pages one at a time.

Adam smiled. Seeing the happiness in George's face made all the box-carrying worthwhile. It wasn't every day that he got to see genuine joy in someone's face.

Adam watched as George flipped page after page onto the table. After he had gone through a few, something caught Adam's eye. At first he thought he was dreaming, but after a few seconds it registered.

"Stop!" he said, and George did.

"Go back a couple of pages," said Adam.

George gave him a strange look and started picking pages back up again. After he picked two off the pile, Adam asked him to stop again. To Adam, the next picture stuck out like a coffee bean on a pile of sugar, but George and Kevin didn't know why.

Adam's eyes widened as he realized what he saw.

George had drawn the symbol Adam had seen in the fake Heartstone.

CHAPTER FOUR

George had a puzzled look on his face as he glanced at the drawing and back to Adam. Even Kevin looked confused.

"What is that?" asked Adam as he pointed to the paper.

The picture on the paper looked like a round figure eight with a triangular hourglass shape inside of it. A short line cut across the point where the two lobes and triangles intersected.

"...I...I don't know," said George. "It's just a doodle I couldn't get out of my head."

Adam paused before deciding to tell George why he was so interested in the picture.

"Do you know about everything that happened here last year?" asked Adam.

George nodded. "I've been told what happened in the Radome caves."

"Did you also hear about the fake Heartstone and the message inside of it?" Adam asked again.

George's eyes narrowed. "I heard about the fake Heartstone, but nothing about a message. What does that have to do with my drawing?"

"When I connected with the fake Heartstone, there was a message inside saying that the real Heartstone had been stolen. I saw *that* picture at the end of the message," said Adam, pointing at the drawing. "I had assumed it was the symbol of whoever took it."

George looked confused. "How can that be? I saw this in a dream and couldn't get it out of my head. It wouldn't let me sleep so Elianora suggested that I draw it to get it out. I've got no idea where I would have seen this before," he said.

"Did *she* recognize it?" asked Adam.

"If she did, she hid it well," George replied.

Silence filled the kitchen as each of them was lost in deep thought.

"Have *you* talked to her about it?" Kevin asked Adam.

Adam thought it over for a moment. "I described it to her that night, and she didn't say anything about it. I forgot about it until after we heard about the escape, so I asked her again. That time she just told me it doesn't mean anything and changed the subject."

"So you think she knows more than she's saying, then?" asked Kevin.

Adam nodded.

"But how is it in my head?" asked George. "Am I the one who took the Heartstone?" He was visibly disturbed by the thought.

Adam and Kevin looked at each other. They had been thinking the same thing, especially since George used to be Number 2.

Again, they sat in silence. George seemed to become more and more uncomfortable with his thoughts.

Adam could see that it was beginning to really bother George.

"Well," said Adam, "you *were* Number 2 after all, so I would think you would have known a lot of the things that Elianora does. It's probably just a coincidence that this popped up in your mind instead of something else. I don't think it's anything you need to worry about."

George considered this for a few moments and nodded his head, a slight smile returning to his face. "Yeah, you're probably right. I have had quite a lot of things popping into my brain. It's not the first thought that's kept me up at night either."

The sound of noisy brakes bringing an old vehicle to a stop caught everyone's attention and took their mind off of the picture.

"They're back," said Kevin, standing to look out the front window.

"Are you done your drinks?" asked George.

Kevin handed his empty can to George while Adam guzzled the last of his. It burned as he drank it fast, and as soon as it was empty he handed it over to George.

The door opened and in stepped Gurpreet, Jimmy and Mark.

"We're ready for the next load," said Gurpreet.

George held up a finger, signalling Gurpreet to wait, and then pulled a couple of cans of Root Beer out of his fridge.

"We've had our break already," he said, referring to himself, Adam and Kevin. "Now it's your turn."

Mark rushed to the table the second he heard the word break and saw the Root Beer in George's hand. Adam and Kevin left their spots so the others could sit, and George placed a can in front of Mark and Jimmy once they were both seated. When George offered a drink to Gurpreet, Gurpreet thanked him and declined.

"I thought you were all out of Root Beer," said Mark.

George smiled. "I have hiding spots you don't know about Mark," he said in reply.

Gurpreet shook his head at Mark, then spoke to Adam and Kevin. "Since you've had a break, let's continue hauling boxes."

They nodded and followed George to the remaining items. After another half an hour of hauling and sorting, George informed them they were done.

"I can't thank you all enough," he kept saying, almost teary-eyed.

"No problem, George," said Gurpreet, "but do you need any more help? It is your first day back here in over a year? You probably need some groceries."

George considered this for a moment. "Yes, I guess I probably do," he said slowly.

"Well," said Gurpreet, "How about this: I'll take Kevin and Adam with me to the dump, since I took Mark and Jimmy last time,"

Mark did a fist pump and said, "yesssss," happy to get out of that job.

"Meanwhile, Mark and Jimmy can take you to the store and carry all of your groceries back here while we're gone." Gurpreet ended the sentence with a big smile watching Mark's fist pumping end abruptly.

George looked like he was trying to make a difficult decision. Gurpreet must have understood why.

"The League is paying for everything you need. The store already knows that. You just make sure you get *everything* you need – food, soap, paper towels – everything. You have help, so use it."

Mark groaned, maybe a bit too loud. Gurpreet gave him a stern look.

George looked as if he were about to cry until Gurpreet held up his hand in a stop signal.

"The only condition is that you have to help the League if we need you, Ok? You don't remember this, but you were one of the most generous people when you were Number 2, so this is just a small bit of payback."

George controlled himself somewhat, but still looked like he was fighting his emotions. He nodded in agreement, unable to speak.

It was at that point that Adam realized just how much George must have gone through in the last year. He felt sorry for George and determined that he would help in any way that he could.

"Well, let's get going," Gurpreet said to Adam and Kevin, "These guys have to get to the store."

Adam and Kevin headed to the door while Mark grumbled behind them. Adam chuckled to himself after hearing Mark, wondering if Mark would ever learn to be quiet when work was being assigned by his dad.

They hopped in the old truck with Adam in the middle next to Gurpreet and Kevin beside the door. Gurpreet slid into the driver's seat and slammed the door shut. The old metal hinges squealed in resistance. He started the engine, which ran smooth although loud, and shifted the truck into gear. Soon, they were driving past Town Hall on their way to the dump, a mile south of town.

Adam couldn't help thinking about George's drawing during the short ride to the dump. How was it stuck in George's mind? George must have been involved with that group in some way, either with it or against it, because of the trouble it was causing him to sleep.

Arriving at the dump, Gurpreet backed the truck up to a deep pit in the ground that contained all of the other papers George had collected. They hopped out and began throwing the remaining boxes on top, but Adam was stuck in thought about George and the symbol – almost obsessing about it.

When they had finished, Gurpreet got back in the truck and pulled it away from the pit while Adam and Kevin waited. While he was in the cab of the truck, Gurpreet fiddled with the glove box for a moment before returning to the edge of the pit. He was carrying a box of wooden matches.

With a quick strike and throw of the match, the pile of papers began to burn. Old dry paper, having been stored indoors for years, started on fire easily and grew up to a large fire in a short amount of time.

"We should have brought some hot dogs," said Gurpreet with a smile.

Kevin nodded back with a big grin on his face. Adam tried to do the same, but only managed a small smile. Gurpreet noticed right away.

"What's wrong, Adam," he asked.

Adam wasn't sure if he should say anything, but decided to ask.

"Well, when you were at the dump the first time, George showed us some of his drawings," replied Adam.

Gurpreet caught on right away. "And one of them was the symbol you saw in the fake Heartstone," Gurpreet finished the sentence for him.

Adam nodded, not completely surprised that Gurpreet already knew about the drawing.

"I forgot that he had his drawings with him and might show them to you," Gurpreet continued.

"Can you tell me anything about that symbol? What does it mean? What does it stand for?" asked Adam.

Gurpreet paused in thought, staring Adam in the eyes the whole time, making Adam uncomfortable.

"Hop in the truck," he said, jerking his thumb in its direction. He was avoiding answering any of Adam's questions.

Adam and Kevin looked at each other. Kevin's eyes widened a little, and the two boys did as Gurpreet asked.

Gurpreet stayed outside and watched the fire for a couple of minutes while the boys waited. Adam decided that Gurpreet was making sure the fire was dying down so that it didn't jump out and start a grass fire when they left.

Adam looked at Kevin and Kevin shrugged. For some reason, they felt that they should stay quiet until Gurpreet said they could speak again.

Once the flames had died down, Gurpreet got back in the truck. He started the engine and they drove away, but once they reached the main grid road Gurpreet turned south instead of north toward town.

Adam was pretty sure he knew where they were going.

In a few minutes, the truck scraped its way through the tree tunnel leading to Elianora's farm. Adam was nervous that his questions were getting him in trouble, as Gurpreet maintained a stoic silence the entire way.

When they stopped, Gurpreet finally spoke.

"I was told that if I heard you asking about the symbol again, I should bring you out to see her, so here we are." He waved the boys out of the cab.

Kevin opened the door and stepped out, and Adam shuffled his way across the seat following close behind. Gurpreet remained in the truck.

"Just go in and tell her you saw the symbol at George's. I have to go back and make sure the fire dies completely, but I'll come pick you up in half an hour, ok?"

The look on Gurpreet's face made Adam nervous as he nodded in agreement. Gurpreet noticed and changed his expression to a smile.

"Don't worry – she just wants to talk to you."

Adam nodded again and closed the door, but Gurpreet's sudden change in mood didn't do anything to help the knot in Adam's gut.

The truck motor cranked to a start, and Gurpreet eased the truck back out the way he came. Adam looked to the house and then to Kevin.

"After you," he said.

"Gurpreet didn't say she wanted to talk to *me*, so, after *you*," Kevin replied.

Adam would have liked it if Kevin led the way, but he could tell that it wasn't going to happen that time. He took a deep breath, held for a moment and exhaled it all again before turning toward the house and beginning to walk. Kevin followed close behind.

He knocked on the porch door, stepped inside and called "Hello?"

"Come downstairs," Elianora called from far away.

The boys took off their shoes and followed the voice. At the bottom of the stairs, the sliding door was propped open and they could see Elianora inside the cave beyond. She was sitting in a rocking chair near her bookshelf with a book in hand, reading. As they stepped into the cave, they noticed that all of her things were back to where they had been the first time they had seen the area.

She looked up at the boys and smiled. "Sorry, I just want to finish the last part of this book." She held up a finger for the boys to wait, flipped a page, read it quickly and closed the book.

"That was quite good," she said.

She held the book up for the boys to see. They had expected her to be reading one of the books from her own library – the ones with strange writing on the spine -but the book she held up was a surprise. It was "Harry Potter and the Chamber of Secrets."

"Have you read this?" she asked.

Adam shook his head while Kevin nodded.

"I've read the first four," said Kevin, "but the fifth one has been gone from the library for a long time. I'm just waiting for it to get returned."

Adam looked at Kevin like he was seeing someone new.

"What?" Kevin replied to Adam's stare. "Didn't think I could read a novel?"

"No, actually, I didn't," Adam stated with a straight face. A few moments later, he smiled and chuckled a little.

"So, why have you stopped in for a visit?" asked Elianora.

Adam looked at Kevin and back to Elianora as he remembered why they were there. "Well, Gurpreet dropped us off here to talk to you about the symbol I saw in the Heartstone."

Elianora nodded, her expression looking more solemn. "I heard the old town truck, but thought it was Gurpreet coming to ask me something. I knew it couldn't have been Don Chen because he's away on holidays. I was surprised to hear you two walking up after it pulled away."

"You heard it from down here?" asked Kevin.

Elianora nodded. "That truck is pretty loud, you have to admit. And the sound is quite distinct. The squealing brakes give it away every time."

Adam agreed with her.

"So, why the sudden interest in that symbol again?" she asked.

"Well," replied Adam, "We were helping clean out George's place and saw his drawings."

She nodded, her face showing understanding. "I didn't think you would get a chance to see his drawings with all the work to be done there. Oh well." She shrugged her shoulders.

"What does it mean? Did George have something to do with the disappearance of the Heartstone?" asked Adam.

Kevin nodded along as Adam spoke.

Elianora pointed to a spot near her on the floor where the rocks were high enough to sit. "Come, take a seat."

They obeyed, and as soon as they were seated she began.

"Do you know what the symbol of the Sentinel League represents?" she asked.

Adam hadn't really thought about it until that point, but realized it must have some sort of meaning. He shook his head.

Kevin spoke up, "I can't see what a bowtie has to do with anything I've learned so far."

Elianora smiled. "That's because it isn't a bowtie, contrary to what most people believe. Do you have your lapel pin on you?" she asked Adam.

He shook his head. "I hid it because I haven't needed it much since last year and I don't want to lose it."

Elianora smiled. "That's probably a good idea," she said. She stood up and walked across the room, shuffling through a stack of books until she found the one she was looking for. She returned to her seat flipping through pages, stopping abruptly at one and turning it for the boys to see. It was a drawing of the lapel pin, still looking mostly like a bowtie to the boys.

"Yes, it does look like a bowtie like this," she said. "But, what does it look like when I do this?" She turned the book ninety degrees.

It took a moment, but Adam couldn't believe he didn't see it before.

"It's an hourglass," he replied.

Elianora smiled and nodded.

Kevin said, "Oh yeah, I see it too."

"Exactly. It is an hourglass, but it's meant to be on its side. Any ideas why?" she continued.

Kevin replied this time. "If you turn an hourglass on its side, the sand doesn't flow anymore. Is that a symbol for time standing still?"

"Very good, Kevin," said Elianora. "Mankind came up with this symbol for us a long time ago, mainly because the Teneo don't seem to age – therefore, our time stands still from their point of view."

"We had a class in school for a whole year and they said nothing about that," said Adam. "Why wouldn't that be one of the first things they teach?"

"That's because not everyone knows about it. If we had to teach everything that ever happened in the Sentinel League you wouldn't have time for other school work." She replied as she closed the book and set it on her lap.

Adam felt as if she were skirting the question, but decided to let it pass.

"So, now that we know about the hourglass on its side, what about that other symbol?" Adam continued to press for an answer.

"That is another story in itself. It's actually full of meaning, but I'll give you the quick summary. The symbol isn't nearly as old as the Sentinel League symbol, only about a hundred and fifty years or so. Anyway, somewhere in the early 1800's, a group started forming within the Sentinel League made up of some of the senior members who were scientists and scholars in the organization. They felt that if they could study us, they could learn the secret of our long lives and use it to lengthen their own. They called themselves 'Aeturnum', meaning 'eternal', since they were looking for eternal life."

Adam nodded, having already wondered about the same thing in the past.

"We agreed to let them examine us, and even went so far as letting them do experiments on us. They did everything they could at the time and came up with nothing. They even tried using our blood in transfusions on themselves, but it didn't work. They found nothing unusual, and after years of trying, they abandoned the idea. Years later, in the mid 1900's, we began testing ourselves and trying to unlock the secret to our health and long lives. So far, we have found nothing."

Adam was confused. "But the Teneo have all this knowledge and technology. You must be further along than us in medical knowledge, aren't you?"

Elianora nodded. "Yes, for most of history we have been, but Mankind has been catching up quite quickly in the last hundred years. Our last and best medical researcher was killed at that time, and none of the remaining Teneo are in that field, so we've relied on Mankind's advances in medicine."

Adam had a thought, although it was off-topic. "How many Teneo are left?" he asked.

Elianora raised an eyebrow. "Well, including Larix and myself, there are 11."

Adam was surprised at this low number. "How many of you were there?"

"I believe you would like to know how many there were in total at the peak," she corrected him.

He nodded his head.

"Twenty-six," she continued.

"*That's all*?" asked Kevin, surprised. "Didn't any of you get married and have any kids?"

"Well, one of the costs of a long life seems to be the inability to reproduce. None of us were ever able to have children."

Adam was sad to hear that. From all the time he had spent with Elianora, he felt that she would be a great parent, like Kevin's parents. It was a shame that someone so capable wouldn't have the opportunity.

"What happened to all of the others?" asked Kevin.

"Well, when our home island disappeared there were 11 of us that disappeared with it. Three more have been killed by Larix directly and one more by the Heartstone indirectly."

"That one was the explosion in Halifax harbour, right?" asked Kevin.

Elianora nodded.

"How many were Decreta?" asked Adam.

"Only five, if you include Larix."

The news was interesting to Adam, but he remembered the reason he was there and got back on track.

"Why would a group whose concern is finding a way to have a longer life by studying the Teneo want an object that kills Teneo?"

Elianora shrugged. "Well, it's a very powerful object. Don't forget, it wasn't just used to kill Teneo. Larix was able to do many things with it, like making Mount Vesuvius erupt for instance. Many people would love to figure out how it works and make a weapon out of it. Even though Aeturnum began looking for a way to extend life, I'm not sure they wouldn't want to build a weapon if they had the chance. In the past they have studied it in many different ways, from finding its effects on plants and animals to trying to find its power source and harness it for clean energy. It seems to regenerate on its own and leave no waste, so that would be a wonderful power source. On the other hand, though, it could be used to develop terrible weapons. Just look at nuclear energy. It is a relatively clean source of energy, but in the wrong hands it can cause massive devastation. Aeturnum has never been able to activate it as a power source, though, but they'd like to keep trying. So far, the only person who has ever been able to use it is Larix, and we don't even have a hunch why."

Adam thought that sounded reasonable, but he still had questions. "So why would the Aeturnum symbol be stuck in George's mind? Do you think he was part of stealing the Heartstone?"

Elianora smiled and shook her head. "No. I don't think he had anything to do with it. I've known him for most of his life, and it would go against his nature. He's always been very kind and generous to everyone. Even after he lost his memory, his major concern was the safety of everyone in town – even if some of the kids called him crazy." She looked right at Kevin, who hung his head feeling a little ashamed.

"So, how did George lose his memory anyway?" asked Adam.

"As you know, people who don't make it as initiates have some of their memory erased. It doesn't happen very often, but when it does, we have a very effective method of doing so. I won't bore you with the details, but we can take a person back to just before the point in time they find out about the League. Usually it hasn't been very long since they were initiated, so they don't lose much time and it isn't very traumatic. George performed the procedure on an initiate by himself and somehow it worked on George as well as the initiate. The initiate only lost a couple of weeks of memory, but George lost years.

The funny thing about it is that it didn't work perfectly on George. He still had parts of it floating around in his head. That's what made him keep chasing after the Sentinel League."

"Why didn't you just tell him about it again and re-train him?" asked Kevin.

"We tried. Somehow, anything we taught George about the League would cause a reaction. It seemed that he would reset again whenever he learned too much about the League. That's why we ended up putting him where he is and took care of him, letting him go about his business. Every couple of years he would learn enough about the league that it would cause a reset."

"So how come he remembers it now?" asked Adam.

"The gas that Larix used to make everyone a zombie seemed to open a door to his memories. The mental blocks he had are going away with time. The gas gave Larix just enough of an opening that he was able to confirm that Grayson was one of the sites where we kept the Heartstone and that I was living here. It's only been the past month that his memories have started returning and staying, though. I've been working with George to recover as much of his memory as possible since then, but most of it is still locked. I don't want to overload him, so we haven't discussed Aeturnum yet. It confuses him when some of the images come up, but he's gotten much better at dealing with it. That's why he's back at his home now."

"But why would Aeturnum be bothering him unless he had some connection to it?" asked Adam.

"You'd be surprised by what has bothered him. Whenever he has a panic attack I've gotten him to draw whatever is bothering him, and it's been everything from a puppy to a toothbrush. None of it makes any sense. I'm pretty sure that it is just a random image that came to his mind, that's all. He knew all about Aeturnum because they kept asking him for access to the Heartstone when he was Number 2, and before he became Number 3 he worked at our school teaching initiates about Aeturnum as part of our history, so I'm not surprised at all. You shouldn't think too much into it either,"

Still, Adam felt that Elianora knew much more than she was saying, but he decided not to push the issue. He nodded in agreement.

"Besides, I'm not too concerned about it, so neither should you be. But since you're here and we're on the topic of the Heartstone, I have a little job for you."

Adam looked at her with curiosity. "Sure. What do you need me to do for you?"

"It has to do with what I told you before I sent you into the tunnels when Larix first showed up here."

"Brutus?" asked Adam.

His mind brought back the memory of that moment. Elianora was rushing them back into the tunnels when she decided to give Adam the strange instruction. "If something happens to me, go find Brutus in Killaly," she had whispered in his ear.

In the excitement of the moment, it didn't seem that strange, but on second thought a year later he wondered why she had made the comment.

Kevin looked confused.

"Yes, Brutus."

"Sure. What do you need me to do?"

"I need you to try and get an Impression Stone from Brutus," she said.

Now Adam looked as confused as Kevin.

"Wouldn't it be easier to send one of the senior members to get it?" he asked again.

"Gurpreet and Don have tried, but haven't been able to get it. I think you might have more luck."

"Can't *you* get it?" he asked.

She shrugged. "Possibly, but I'd like *you* to try. I haven't been too concerned about it, because I know the message it contains."

"How?" asked Adam.

"I put the instructions into it, of course."

That made sense to Adam. For some reason he hadn't thought about it, but realized that someone would have had to put the instructions into the Impression Stones.

"Now that Larix has been through every trap we have, the information on the stone isn't that important, but they are rare and hard to come by, so I'd like to get it back to use again."

"So you think that *I* can find it?" asked Adam, unsure of himself.

Elianora nodded. "It's worth a try. If you don't find it, don't worry too much. The men have a baseball game in Killaly tomorrow, so I thought you could catch a ride with Gurpreet. I'll let him know."

"I still don't understand why I'd have better luck than the others," asked Adam.

Elianora paused and smiled. "I was getting to that. Everyone has talents in one area or another. You just happen to have a few talents that you might not know about yet. You see, your Grandpa and your Dad had mechanical talents like you, as well as talents with nature – the reason you have such deep connections with the Kurling stones. Your Grandpa is the one who hid the

Impression Stone with Brutus to begin with and your Dad was the last one to give it back."

"But how does that make it easier for me to get the Impression Stone?" asked Adam.

Elianora thought for a moment before speaking. "Because there's a trick to making Brutus give it up, and your relatives could do it. You like to take things apart and try and build new things out of them, right?"

Adam nodded, not understanding where she was going.

"Do you find yourself visualizing the internal parts in your head sometimes before you even take something apart?"

Adam thought about it again and nodded. It seemed natural to him.

"Well, in the same way that you connected with the stones in Kurling, I'm betting you have the ability to 'connect' with mechanical devices – to understand them better than most, even with out taking them apart. I think that's a key to getting Brutus to talk."

Adam had never thought of it that way before, but it made sense.

"I need you to try something, though. You need to try and connect with a mechanical object in the same way you connect with a Kurling stone, but you need a couple of tips from me in order to do it. First, you need to be in contact with whatever object you are examining. Usually it is best to make contact with your hands as far apart as you can on the object. Next you need to close your eyes and really focus *inside* the object. Don't *push* yourself into it; *pull* it to you until you are inside. As long as you maintain contact and with enough focus, you will 'see' inside whatever object you are connected to – at least, that's the way I've heard it described. I'm mainly connected to nature, myself. Never had a mechanical knack. So when you go home today, find something and give it a try. Practice on a few things before you go to Killaly."

Adam didn't know if he should be excited by the possibility he might have this talent or worried that Elianora had gone a little crazy.

"So my dad was able to 'connect' with mechanical things?" asked Adam.

Elianora nodded. "Yes. He was good at it. It was almost a curse though because any time anyone had a mechanical problem they called him to fix it immediately. Because he liked to help people, he had a hard time refusing. It annoyed your mother because he always seemed to be gone helping everyone else."

"Do I have any hidden talents?" asked Kevin.

Elianora turned to him and nodded. "Everyone does, and everyone has talents in many areas," she began, "but some people have deeper talent than others. Some find their talents early, while others search their entire lives and never find just the right one. I have no doubt that you are one who has deep talent in some area; I am just not sure which one yet. Your family line is deeply connected with nature – hence them all being farmers for the last few generations."

Kevin smiled after hearing this explanation.

"So, can I count on you to try?" Elianora asked Adam.

Adam nodded.

"Good. And perfect timing too. Gurpreet is on his way back here."

Adam and Kevin strained to hear the truck, but could not. They looked at each other and shrugged.

AETURNUM

"Let's go meet him. He's only a few minutes away. I need to tell him something anyway," said Elianora. She stood up from her chair, placed the book on the bookshelf and followed the boys up the stairs.

By the time they were outside, they could hear a truck approach on the gravel road, then the squeal of the brakes, and finally the scraping of trees on the side of the truck. The rusty vehicle pulled up beside the group soon after.

Adam and Kevin slid in next to Gurpreet and closed the door. Elianora was at the driver's window, talking to Gurpreet.

"This morning's report confirmed a sighting of Larix yesterday in South Africa," she said. "Just thought I'd let you know."

Gurpreet nodded, "Thanks. Always good to know. See ya."

They waved goodbye to Elianora and started heading back. Gurpreet navigated them back through the trees and onto the road before anyone said anything.

"So, did she explain everything to you?" asked Gurpreet.

They nodded.

"I just don't understand how Aeturnum would steal the Heartstone," said Adam.

"That hasn't been confirmed," replied Gurpreet. "Don't worry about it too much though. We've got a lot of really good people working on it as we speak."

Adam and Kevin nodded, returning back to silence. Adam's mind went back to the task Elianora had given him – finding Brutus and getting the Impression Stone back.

"Gurpreet," he said, feeling strange for not having called him 'Mr. Gupta', "Elianora asked me to hitch a ride with the men's baseball team to Killaly tomorrow."

Gurpreet chuckled. "She's wants you to try and find the Impression Stone, right?"

Adam nodded, but wondered why Gurpreet chuckled.

"Did she tell you anything about where it is?" Gurpreet asked.

"Only that I need to find Brutus in order to get it."

Gurpreet grinned. "I'll give you a ride tomorrow, and I'll introduce you to Brutus myself. I hope you have better luck than the rest of us at getting Brutus to talk."

Adam had the feeling that there was a lot more to the story than he had been told so far.

CHAPTER FIVE

By the time Adam had arrived at home that evening Mary was home already. After he ate and finished the dishes Mary had more work for him to do. The remainder of the evening was spent washing and folding his laundry including his bedding. That work on top of the physical labor at George's exhausted him, sending him to sleep much earlier than usual. He completely forgot that he was supposed to try connecting with something mechanical.

It was a poor sleep, filled with odd dreams. For some reason, he dreamed that he was holding Mark's head and trying to 'see' inside it in the way Elianora had told him. In the dream, Mark was really a robot and Adam needed to know how he worked but didn't want to take his head apart. After trying multiple times to 'see' inside, Adam gave up and took out a hacksaw. He was about to make the first cut into Mark's forehead when he bolted up in bed, wide awake.

As soon as he grasped that it was only a dream, he realized that he had forgotten to try 'seeing' into something mechanical. After looking at the clock, though, he decided that it was way too early in the morning to do that yet. Instead he tried to force himself back to sleep by wondering what *really was* in Mark's head. It made him chuckle as he pictured Mark's brain sitting on a small couch, watching a cartoon through Mark's eyes while it sipped a small can of Root Beer. Every time it took a sip, Mark's body would take a sip from its own can. This strange spectacle managed to tie up Adam's thoughts long enough that he drifted off to sleep with a smile on his face.

When he woke again, the first thing he remembered was the task that Elianora had given him. As soon as he had dressed, he rummaged through the dresser drawer where he kept his projects, but the only thing he could find was the flashlight he had built the previous summer. Because *he* had built it, he knew exactly what it looked like on the inside, so he couldn't be sure if he was really connected to it or if he was just remembering what he had already seen.

Looking around the room he didn't immediately notice anything that he could try to look inside until his eyes settled on the old alarm clock beside his bed. While his friends had alarm clocks that either held their phones or were infinitely programmable digital devices, Adam had an old-school alarm that looked like it came out of a cartoon from the 1950's. It had a large round face with big numbers on the front and two large bells on top with a striker in the middle. When the hour hand reached the imprecise position of the alarm hand, the striker would ring the two bells on top, as long as he remembered to wind it up the night before since it wasn't battery powered.

He grabbed the clock and looked at it, excited at the possibility of this new talent. With a hand on each side, he closed his eyes and concentrated. He imagined that his mind left his head and ran down his arm. When it tried to enter the clock nothing happened. He saw it pulling on the front dial to get in, but soon realized that he was just imagining things and not really connecting at all.

He opened his eyes and stared at the clock, then remembered connecting with the Kurling stones, so he brought the clock up until it touched the bridge of his nose between his eyes. He held it and concentrated for what seemed like minutes, but again nothing happened, so he put the clock down

Sitting on his bed disappointed, he wondered if Elianora was wrong and that he didn't inherit the talent. After all, he had never connected with any of the items he worked on before, and he *had* spent hundreds of hours working on that stuff.

After some thought he decided that one failed attempt didn't mean he wouldn't be able to ever do it, just that it may not be as easy as he hoped, so he thought about the other items he could try. The TV would be fun, but Mary wouldn't be too happy if she caught him touching her favorite thing. He would have to find something else.

As his mind moved through the house and saw nothing to try, it made its way outside and into his garage. Up on the back shelf it saw an item that it thought might work.

Once his mind had drifted back into his head again, he made his way downstairs. Mary didn't have to work that day, so Adam wasn't sure if she'd still be in bed or in front of her TV. As he reached the bottom of the stairs, he saw that she was the latter.

"Good morning," said Adam, although he tried to stay quiet. Mary nodded back in his general direction.

Adam poured himself a glass of milk and downed it fast while he looked out the kitchen window. It was raining, so when he finished drinking and putting his cup in the sink, he grabbed his jacket, opened the door and stepped outside. After a sprint to the garage through the light misty rain, he shook the water from his hair and stamped his feet to dry his shoes a little, even though it was just a dirty old garage.

Up on the back shelf sat an old plastic radio, the one he had seen when his mind wandered out to the garage earlier. It was one of the first transistor radios available many years ago, but also one of the cheapest ones ever made. It worked when it wanted to, and on some clear nights Adam could pick up the odd radio station. One night he had picked up a station that was playing stories from the past, back when people didn't have screens to stare at endlessly and actually liked listening to adventures on the airwaves. He enjoyed sitting in his chair and imagining the old western story streaming from the noisy speaker. That night, he fell asleep in his garage, only to wake in the morning with nothing but static coming from the radio.

At that moment Adam thought the radio would be a great object to try and look inside. It was one of the few items around that he had never taken apart, although he didn't know why not, but just then he was glad he didn't. Since he had no idea what it would look like inside, it was the perfect object to test.

After taking the radio from the shelf, he sat in his usual spot and set the radio on the table. He closed his eyes and concentrated, then put his hands on both sides of the radio. He focused on getting into the radio for a few minutes, letting go and sitting back in his chair with a sigh.

It hadn't worked. He hadn't been able to look into the radio at all. There wasn't even a hint of a connection with it, the same as the clock in his room. He was disappointed that he didn't inherit this particular talent from his father because it would have been another connection that he and Edward could have shared.

Feeling kind of gloomy, he sat back in his chair and closed his eyes for a while, trying to get his mind off of the disappointment of failing to see inside the radio. It was getting close to 9 am, so he distracted himself by wondering what Kevin, Jimmy, and Mark were doing. Kevin was probably working with his Dad on the farm. Mark was most likely still sleeping, as he liked to brag about constantly. Jimmy was the only one that probably wasn't busy, but he was likely still sleeping too. Adam thought that maybe he could ride over in the rain and see if Jimmy was awake, but changed his mind as the rain pounded harder on the old garage roof.

With the increase in water, the roof showed a few leaks near the front edge of the garage. Adam decided to try and patch as much as he could from the inside using a pail of tar he had found at the dump. He moved his old step-stool to the front of the garage and opened the pail. The tar inside smelled terrible, but it did the trick. After working it into the edge of the roof where it was leaking, he continued tarring the entire front roofline – since he was halfway done already.

When he finished, he put everything away and headed for the house so that he could clean his hands and maybe have an early lunch. As soon as he stepped inside the house, Mary smelled the tar.

"Make sure you don't make a big mess in the sink," she told him as he walked past.

"Yes mom," he replied. He grabbed the dish soap from the kitchen first, because he knew the hand soap they had in the bathroom wouldn't be strong enough to take the tar off. Even the dish soap wouldn't work too well without a lot of hot water.

Once his hands were clean and he had made sure there were no remnants in the sink, Adam went to the fridge to get some food. He made himself a buttered bologna sandwich with the last piece of bologna and crust pieces of bread, then chased it down with a glass of something made from cheap powdered drink mix – pomegranate pineapple possibly.

"Mom, we're out of bread and meat," he said.

"I knew I forgot something yesterday," she replied. "I'll get more this afternoon."

Adam grabbed his damp rain jacket again and headed back out to the garage. As soon as he sat back down, the sound of rain on the roof let up a lot but still continued in a soft drizzle.

Adam picked up the radio and stared at it once more. *Why won't you let me look inside?* he wondered. Again, he closed his eyes and concentrated on seeing the inside, and again it didn't work. He set the radio back on the coffee table and sat back in the chair, frustrated.

A little while later, the door to the garage opened and in stepped Kevin. He was wearing a big yellow rain jacket and rubber boots. He shook the rain from the jacket and pulled back the hood.

"I thought you'd be in here. That's why I didn't call on the phone. Thought I might wake your mom. She wouldn't be too happy if I did."

Adam smiled and nodded. "Good thinking. She's up, but she could have still been in bed. You're not working today?"

Kevin shook his head. "Nope. Fed the cattle this morning and sat around watching TV. Now I'm free until later tonight. I thought I would drag you over to my place for a while. It's supposed to stop raining soon."

Adam cheered up at Kevin's invitation.

AETURNUM

"Sure. Sounds a lot better than what I was doing," Adam looked to the old radio.

"No way!" exclaimed Kevin. "Did you do it? What did you see?"

Adam frowned and shook his head. "Nope. Nothing. I tried my alarm clock this morning and then this radio."

Kevin was quiet for a few seconds. "Maybe you just need to keep trying."

Adam gave a chuckle. "Just don't tell me the story of 'The Little Engine That Could'," he said.

Kevin smiled and rolled his eyes. "Whatever. You know what I mean. Elianora said it isn't the easiest thing to do, so maybe you need to practice. Try it again," he said, pointing at the radio as he sat down next to Adam.

"Yes sir, Mr. Baranov sir," replied Adam as though he were in the army replying to a senior officer.

Kevin laughed. "Hurry up or I'll make you drop and give me 20 push-ups."

Adam had a smile on his face as he shook his head and picked up the radio. He cleared his throat and closed his eyes, concentrating on the next attempt. He could feel Kevin watching him, which didn't help his concentration at all. After a minute of trying, he put the radio back down.

"Nothing," he said.

Kevin scratched his head. "The only thing I remember from Elianora yesterday is that she said you're not supposed to try and push your mind into it, you're supposed to pull it to you – whatever that means. It seemed strange. That's why I remember it."

Kevin's observation triggered Adam's memory. Kevin was right; that's exactly what Elianora had said. Each

59

time Adam had tried that morning, he was forcing his thoughts into the radio, not trying to pull it to him. The realization that he hadn't been doing it like Elianora had said got him excited that it could still work.

"I hate to admit it, but you're right. I've been doing it wrong so far. Let me give it another try," said Adam.

Adam picked up the radio once more. He closed his eyes and began to concentrate, but this time he didn't picture his mind going out to the radio. He concentrated on bringing the radio to his mind. A flash went off, causing the eye in his mind to blink, and when he opened it again he was inside. His heart jumped at the realization.

"I'm in," he said.

"No. Way." replied Kevin.

Adam had taken apart enough electronics to realize what he was seeing, but the way he was seeing it was quite unique. Tiny three-legged transistors stood like water towers in front of him. A capacitor to the left looked like a flat-roofed grain bin on the prairie. It was an amazing sight! He turned to look left and another flash went off. He opened his eyes and he was back looking at the radio held in his hands again.

"That was so weird and cool at the same time," said Adam.

"You weren't in there for long," said Kevin.

"I got excited and lost concentration," he replied.

"Then get un-excited and get back in there," said Kevin, "and don't talk this time. I'll try not to talk either."

Adam nodded at Kevin and returned to the radio. That time, it was easy to get back inside. He started at the same point as the first time but then glided along while looking around. He realized that he only had to *want* to move in a direction and he would float that way. As he moved he saw a long cylinder with wire coiled around it, but it looked the size of a fuel tanker you would see driving down the highway. On top of it was a large metal rod tied to a huge off-white coloured rope. The rope led away from the rod in both directions and each end looped around a massive pulley before meeting above. Where the ends of the rope met, they were tied to another metal rod resting against some glass. On the glass there were numbers printed in reverse, like looking at them in a mirror. The numbers started at 500 and went up to 1300. It was the indicator for the station! One of the pulleys must have been turned by the tuning knob on the outside and it moved the metal rod along the coiled cylinder to tune in the stations. Adam noticed that there was a lot of junk built up around the metal rod where it met the coil, and that was probably why it didn't pick up the radio signals very well.

Adam flashed back to reality with a big smile on his face.

"Kicked out again?" asked Kevin.

"Nope. I kicked myself out," he replied. "I think I saw why this thing isn't working great, so we're going to take it apart. I want to make sure I wasn't just dreaming about being in there."

Kevin nodded. "Go to it."

Adam got up and went over to his toolbox, returning with various screwdrivers. He sat down, flipped the radio on its face and started removing the screws from the back cover.

"What was it like?" asked Kevin.

"It was cool. I could see all the parts, but they were huge. The strange part of it was that I know there isn't much light inside, but I saw everything as if there were lights everywhere."

"That would freak me out a little," said Kevin.

"Now that I'm thinking about it, yeah, it is a little freaky," replied Adam.

He took the last screw from the back and popped off the cover. The inside looked exactly like he had seen it, although his view was now from above instead of on the same level as the components.

He found the tuning coil right away and recognized all of the other parts he had seen while inside. The biggest surprise was how small the parts actually were from his normal point of view.

With a lot of care, he used a small paint brush to clean the little metal rod that came in contact with the tuning coil. He blew inside to clean out the dust, and then decided to try plugging the radio in and give it a try.

As soon as he heard some noise coming from the speaker, he fiddled with the dial on the front. In no time he picked up CBC radio near the lowest part of the dial. It came in full and clear.

Adam smiled that the radio was working perfectly. He thought that he should have taken it apart a long time ago since it was that easy of a fix. After a few moments, he realized the possibilities that his new-found talent would bring to him. He could look into things and figure out what was wrong, or at least just see how to get into them with out breaking them open, as he had done many times in the past. Sometimes pulling things apart damaged them more than anything – especially if you didn't know exactly what you were doing.

"If you would've been able to do that when we were stuck in the tunnels the first time, things might have turned out a lot different," said Kevin, referring to the first time they entered the tunnel and were locked on the other side of a sliding door with a sticky mechanism.

Adam chuckled. "That night would have ended differently, but I think the rest would have gone the same. We would have been back in there the next day anyway."

Kevin thought it over and nodded, agreeing with Adam. He stood up and pointed at the door. "Wanna tell your mom where you're going? I have some things at home you can practice on."

Adam agreed and led the way to the house. Kevin stayed outside while Adam popped his head through the door and told Mary what he was doing. He also mentioned that he was going with the Gupta's to the baseball game in Killaly later on if it dried up enough. To his surprise, he didn't receive the usual grunt in reply. Mary actually said, "Ok, see you later."

It seemed strange to Adam, but he didn't think much about it, and soon he was on his way to the Baranov farm.

"I wonder what things you can look inside. Does it have to be mechanical, or does it have to have space inside?" asked Kevin, more as a statement than a question.

"I was wondering the same thing. I'm going to ask Elianora next time I see her, but until then I'll just keep trying different things," replied Adam.

They skirted a large pothole on the gravel road that was filled with dirty rainwater before turning into the Baranov's long driveway.

"What if you could look inside people? You could finally prove if Mark has a brain or not and maybe see if he has some sort of defect that makes him act like he does."

Normally, Adam would have laughed, but he remembered his dream.

"This is freaky! I just had a dream this morning like that," said Adam. He continued by describing the dream in detail.

Kevin laughed. "I don't think it's too freaky. Everyone wonders what's going on in Mark's head. We just happened to come up with it at the same time today."

That made Adam laugh as they stepped up to the Baranov's side door. Little footsteps seemed to be drawn to Adam's laughter, and a second later Karlea skidded to a stop at the doorway leading to the kitchen.

"Hi Adam," she said in a pleasant voice. She turned and ran back in the direction she had come from just as quickly as she had arrived.

"Hi Karlea...." Adam's voice trailed off since he wasn't fast enough before she ran away.

"She's got more energy than anyone I've ever met," said Kevin. "I keep telling her she must be adopted, 'cause the rest of us are never in that big of a hurry."

"You're adopted," came the reply from Karlea somewhere deeper in the house. Adam was surprised that she had heard Kevin's comment and laughed at how fast her response was.

Karlea's words echoed through the house as they stepped into the kitchen. On the other side of the kitchen and past the dining room table, Adam could see Mike and Charity Baranov relaxing in the living room. Mike had a newspaper open while Charity sat in the rocking chair reading a novel.

"Hi Adam," said Charity. She looked up from her book as the two boys got closer.

"Hi Mrs. Bar...I mean, Charity." Adam felt strange calling his best-friend's mother by her first name.

Charity reached over and smacked Mike's foot, startling him.

"Uh..sorry...hi Adam," he said, peeking his head out from behind the Melville Advance. "Good story in here about the long term effects of the spring runoff," he continued before getting back to his story.

Kevin shook his head. "Dad."

Mike peeked around the paper again.

"Do you have anything broken that you need Adam to look INTO?" said Kevin, stressing the last word to make an impact.

Mike put down the paper and sat up. He looked at Kevin. "Like we discussed last night?" he asked.

Kevin nodded.

Mike looked to Charity, excitement and a smile clear on his face. She stared back at him for a moment, finally nodding and saying, "Go."

Mike looked like a kid that was just told he was going to Disneyland.

"How about us guys take a walk out to the shop?" he said, "I've got a couple of things for you to *look* at."

Adam nodded and followed as Mike slipped past. In a few moments, they were stepping inside Mike's farm shop. It was a newer straight wall steel building that was long and wide, with a huge steel door on the front so Mike was able to drive his equipment inside for repairs. Most of the floor was dirt except for a long narrow cement pad along one side where all of the tools and repair equipment sat.

"I've been wondering if you were going to be able to see into things," said Mike as he rummaged through some parts. "Actually, more like *hoped* you would be able to."

He pulled out a medium-sized electric motor and handed it to Adam.

"Tell me what's wrong with this motor," he said.

Adam felt awkward, but the smile on Mike's face took the edge off.

"I've only done it twice so far, so I hope I don't disappoint you," said Adam.

Mike shook his head. "You won't disappoint me either way. If you did it twice this morning, I'm sure you can do it again. If you fail this time, it just means you need more practice – that's all. There's no pressure here. Just give it a try."

With words like that, Adam couldn't refuse. He took the motor in his hands, closed his eyes and concentrated. He saw the flash and opened his mind's eye again. This time he was in a wide open space, and the silver land under his feet curved down to the right and the left, but travelled straight out ahead and behind him. The low copper coloured ceiling shone above even though he still couldn't find a light source. He looked around and couldn't see anything in particular, but then he noticed a wall far in front of him, so he decided to head in that direction. It looked like a long way away so he concentrated on getting there fast, and in the next instant he was there.

If only you could travel like that in the real world, he thought to himself.

He was at the end of the flat silver surface, and a disgusting smell filled his nose. It was coming from his right, so he moved in that direction. After travelling around the curve a little way, he saw the problem.

Adam snapped out of the motor and smiled. "It's baked," he said to Mike. "The windings on two sections have melted through their coating and must be short-circuiting," he continued.

Mike beamed. "Exactly," he said.

Adam raised an eyebrow in surprise. "You already knew?"

Mike nodded. "I pulled this motor apart myself a few months ago and just kept it for parts. It was a test. You were definitely in there alright."

Mike put the motor back on the pile he had picked it out of in the first place before turning back to Adam.

"You're only the second person I've ever met that can do that. Of course, you've probably figured out that the other person was your dad," he said.

Adam nodded, "Yeah, Elianora told me he could."

"I used to get him over once in a while when something was really stumping me. He always came and never complained, even though his talent was in demand quite often. I had a motor in my grain truck that I thought was gone, but after he looked through it we had it running in no time. He would never take any money or anything for his time, though."

Adam enjoyed hearing the story from Mike. He knew that Mike and Ed had been friends.

"The only other person I ever heard of that could do that was your Grandpa McTaggart. I never did meet him, even though he just lived in Killaly."

Adam was surprised. "My grandpa lived in Killaly?" he asked.

Mike's face matched Adam's surprise. "He was the Mayor for a while. You mean, you didn't know that?"

Adam shook his head.

Mike was clearly stunned by the news. "Well, I don't know what to say."

"Did you know much about him?" asked Adam.

Mike shook his head. "Only what I heard from your dad. I guess he was a pretty strict military man, like his father before him, and your dad wasn't. They didn't get along much, even though your Grandpa designed all of the traps in the Radome caves."

Adam was surprised. "I had no idea. He designed all of the traps?"

"Well, Elianora told him what she wanted them to do and he figured out how to make it happen."

"So did my dad move here because my mom was here?" asked Adam.

Mike shook his head. "I can't believe how little you know about your own family. I only know as much as your dad told me, and he never said much. Your mom and dad only moved here once they were married and he was given the job as Number 3. They met when your dad went away for his training with the League – I think he was 17 at the time – and she was there too. He stayed at the school and worked his way up in the League until they sent him here to become Number 3."

"What happened to my Grandpa? And Grandma? I've seen a picture of them, but they were really young."

"Well, your Grandma died giving birth to your dad. She was pretty old when she had him, that much I know. That's why you don't have any Aunts or Uncles. Your Grandpa died just before they moved back here."

Adam's head was reeling with all of the new information he was taking in about his family. So many questions were being answered that he didn't even realize he wanted to know he wanted answered, but so many more kept popping up to replace them.

"My mom told me they had moved overseas," said Adam.

"She's right, actually. Your Grandpa moved overseas the year before he died. He had gotten re-married soon before it happened. I don't think your dad ever met his wife though, since he didn't go to the wedding or the funeral. Other than that, I don't know much. Like I said, only what your dad would tell me."

Adam nodded. "Thanks."

After a few moments, Kevin broke the awkward silence. "Adam's going to come to the game in Killaly today. The Guptas are giving him a ride. Maybe we can find his Grandpa's old house."

"Right on," replied Mike. "We can use as many cheering fans as we can get."

"Well, I'm supposed to talk to Brutus for Elianora," said Adam, "so I don't know how much of the game I'll get to see."

"She thinks you might be able to get the Impression Stone back?" Mike asked.

"Yeah. That's why she told me about my new 'ability'. She thinks it might help."

Mike nodded. "She's probably right. Have you ever been to Killaly or met Brutus before?"

Adam shook his head.

"Kevin's been to Killaly, but I've never introduced him yet. I'll have to do that after the game. I'm not going to say any more, though. I don't want to ruin the surprise."

Adam and Kevin looked at each other.

"Now you're making me worry," said Adam.

"No no, don't worry at all. There's nothing to worry about," said Mike with a grin.

"Why won't anyone tell me anything about him?"

Mike shrugged. "I guess we're just amused easily," he replied, but didn't continue.

Adam decided to drop the subject of Brutus, as he wasn't getting any more information than he already knew. At least he felt better because Mike wouldn't send him or Kevin into a dangerous situation.

"Do you need me to look at anything else while I'm here?" asked Adam.

Mike shook his head. "Not at the moment. I just wanted to make sure you had the same ability as your dad. If I need you in the future, I know how to find you." Mike pointed at Kevin. "And if I do call you to help, I expect you to take money from me for the work, understand?"

Adam was about to refuse pay, but was stopped by the look on Mike's face.

"You'll have to learn that your time is worth money eventually, so you might as well start now," he finished.

Adam nodded.

"Ok then. Well, I'm going back in to finish reading my paper. You two can hang out here, or whatever you want to do," said Mike. He turned and walked out the door.

"I don't know about you," said Kevin, "but I feel like watching some TV for a while."

"That would be perfect," said Adam, and the two boys headed toward the house.

CHAPTER SIX

The sun came out in the early afternoon and it was hot for once. The water from the morning rain dried up fast, and everyone knew the ball game in Killaly would still be on in the early evening.

Adam and Kevin hung out in the basement watching TV, sometimes interrupted by Karlea and Kelsea playing with their dolls, once by Charity asking them if they needed a snack, and once by Kassie as she was trying to find a private place to talk to Trevor on the phone. Kassie left in a hurry as soon as Kevin started making kissing noises when she got too close. That was when Adam realized that Kevin was much more comfortable with his sister dating Jimmy's older brother than he had been the last year.

The afternoon went by fast and soon Charity called them all upstairs to eat supper, making Adam eat as well. Supper was at 5 o'clock at the Baranov house, and you literally could set a watch by the time Charity called everyone to the table. She assured Adam that there was more than enough, since it was only a simple lasagna.

As Adam chewed the first bite, he knew it wasn't *just* simple lasagna. Simple lasagna came pre-made from the store and tasted like soggy cardboard with bland cheese and tasteless watery sauce inside. Charity's lasagna was amazing! The flavour and texture were unfamiliar to Adam in the best way possible. The noodles were thick and each piece held its shape because the delicious filling was firm and flavourful.

After eating and thanking them for their hospitality once again, Adam headed home to wait for the Gupta's. They would be picking him up at 5:45 pm, since the game was at 6:30. It only took 20 minutes to get to Killaly, so they would arrive in plenty of time for the game.

Adam made it home by 5:35 pm, and as he walked in the door, he realized that his mother had cooked 'something'. The smell was unmistakable. Hot dogs. Normally, this was one of his favourite meals, but after the quality and quantity of lasagna he had just finished, it didn't exactly make his mouth water.

Mary stood at the kitchen counter. She turned when he opened the door.

"I made hot dogs, is that alright?" she asked.

First, Adam was surprised that she had cooked something. Second, he was surprised by the question she asked. He stood in silence, almost in denial that she had asked his opinion so politely.

"You don't want one?" she asked again, sounding slightly upset by his lack of reply as he processed what he saw.

"Uh, sorry. Yeah, for sure. I love hot dogs," Adam replied.

She had gone through the trouble of preparing something for him to eat, so he was going to stuff it down somehow. Adam thought there must have been a sale when she went shopping because there were no hot dogs in the house when he had eaten earlier.

Mary smiled and gave him the plate after squeezing loads of mustard and ketchup on top – just the way Adam would do it for himself. It was even in a real hot dog bun!

They sat at the table and Adam took the first bite. He didn't realize how full he already was until he swallowed the first mouthful. It wasn't going to be easy, but he would finish it quickly and try to seem happy the entire time.

"What did you and Kevin do today?" she asked.

Again, Adam was surprised, but now he was getting suspicious as well.

"Just hung out and watched TV," he replied as he chewed. He wasn't sure if he should tell Mary about his new found talent yet, though. She probably knew about Ed's ability, but he wasn't sure how she would react to him inheriting the same. He decided to keep it a secret for a little while longer.

"The Guptas should be here soon to take me to the ball game in Killaly," said Adam, watching her reaction the entire time. "I should be home by a little after 9."

Mary nodded as Adam took another large bite of his hot dog. He felt like the game he had seen somewhere where you feed a plastic pig food until it's clothes burst, called 'pig goes pop'.

"Thanks for the hot dog," said Adam as he finished the last bite, unsure if he would get it down.

Mary smiled – a rare site for Adam. Now he knew something was up for sure, but he was afraid that if he asked anything the question would make her return to her usual skulking ways, so he said nothing and smiled back at her.

"I'm going out tonight, so I might not be here when you get home. I should be home by midnight," said Mary.

That caught Adam by surprise. Mary never went anywhere or did anything with anyone. And she seemed happy about it too.

"Where are you going?" asked Adam before he realized he didn't want to ask the question.

"Mrs. Garagan and I ended up with free tickets to the dinner theater in Melville tonight," she said. "I haven't been to a dinner theater in forever."

Adam couldn't believe that Mary was excited about going. Up until that point Adam had thought she never liked doing anything that might be considered fun, but the way she spoke about going revealed how much she was looking forward to her evening. She was probably feeling bad that she was going somewhere to have a big meal, so she cooked Adam his favourite food to make up for it. That was unusual for Mary anyway.

Just then a horn honked outside.

"Ok mom. Have fun. Gotta go," he said as he ran his plate to the sink and headed out the door.

The Gupta's dark-grey mini-van was parked out front and the sliding door was already open. Adam hopped in and nodded at Mark who was playing a hand-held video game while wearing headphones. As soon as Adam had his seatbelt fastened, they were on their way.

"So, have you had any luck trying to see into things?" asked Gurpreet.

The question took Adam off guard, but he quickly remembered that Gurpreet *was* Number 2 after all, and had probably spoken at length to Elianora about the possibly of him having that particular talent.

"Actually, yes. It took a while to figure it out, but now I can see into things fairly easily," Adam replied.

Gurpreet nodded. "Very good, very good," he said; his rich East-Indian accent ringing out the words. "We've all tried to persuade Brutus to give us the Impression Stone without any luck. Maybe you can do something with your new talent."

Adam wondered what Gurpreet meant by that. How would the ability to see into objects get some guy named Brutus to tell him anything? Maybe he needed his TV fixed.

"What can you tell me about Brutus?" asked Adam.

Gurpreet looked at Adam in the rear-view mirror. "I think I won't say any more until we get there," he said smiling. "I'll introduce you and let you get started, then pick you up when the game is over if you haven't gotten the stone yet."

Adam nodded, although he would have liked to know more before they arrived. It couldn't be too bad if Gurpreet was willing to drop him off and leave him, could it? He was going to have to wait and find out.

Thankfully, Killaly wasn't a far drive from Grayson. Mark kept his headphones on the entire way, so Adam and Gurpreet made small talk about the baseball game ahead. It was going to be a tough one because a couple of the players weren't able to make it due to prior commitments.

As they turned off the highway and veered onto the angled street leading into the town, Gurpreet slowed down and pointed to the first road leading off to the right.

"The old school and ball diamonds are just half a block up there if you need me before the game is over," he said. "We're just going straight ahead a little way."

Adam watched the buildings on the right pass by, as there was nothing but a row of tall poplar trees on the left with an open field on the other side. He watched ahead and wondered which house belonged to Brutus.

Gurpreet slowed down and parked in front of a building that looked like it had been a gas station at one time. "Here we are," he said, grinning as he unbuckled his seatbelt and opened his door to get out.

Adam followed Gurpreet's lead and got out of the van, but Mark didn't even look up from his game. Adam's eyes roamed around the old building in front of them and he wondered how anyone lived there. It looked abandoned.

Adam walked around the front of the van to meet Gurpreet, but when he got there, Gurpreet wasn't anywhere to be seen. Adam looked around and saw Gurpreet was at the back of the van.

"Are you coming?" he asked as Adam stood there confused.

Adam had assumed they were going into the old gas station, but instead Gurpreet started walking across the street toward the row of trees. After getting his thoughts straight, Adam followed. As he crossed the street, he saw a huge weathered bronze statue of a man on a large pedestal. He was amazed that he had failed to notice it as they pulled up, but he had been looking the other direction under the assumption they were going to someone's house.

Adam hurried across and stopped next to Gurpreet.

Gurpreet looked up at the statue, then at Adam.

"Meet Brutus," he said.

Once again, Adam's brain ground to a halt as he processed this new information and tried to change the direction his mind had been going.

"I'm confused. Am I meeting the guy that this statue is made for?" asked Adam.

Gurpreet chuckled. "No. This *is* the Brutus we want you to meet. I'm glad you are confused because I have been confused about it for a long time now," he replied. "I know we've all been leading you to believe that you were meeting with someone alive. I guess we're easily amused. This statue is of Brutus Killaly, the man who founded the town. He died in 1949, but his statue was put here only 20 years ago. We know that this Brutus is the key to finding the other Impression Stone, but none of us have been able to figure it out. That's where you come in."

Adam raised his eyebrows. "I know Elianora thinks I might be able to figure something out, but if you senior members haven't figured it out, I don't think I can."

"Well, Elianora thinks your ability to see into objects is the key to unlocking this thing."

Adam thought for a moment. "Doesn't she know how to get the stone? I mean, she seems to know everything else."

"She had your Grandpa use his talents to hide the second Impression Stone, but she didn't want to know how he did it. She only wanted a clue. That way, she had a backup just-in-case the other Impression Stone was lost or they couldn't get to it. Your grandpa was a great builder, as was his dad, and they had the ability to see into mechanical things like you, but Elianora doesn't have that ability. She made sure to use people with abilities Larix doesn't have to help hide the stones so that even if he found out where the Heartstone was, he would have a hard time getting to it, as you found out last year. He was just lucky to find you; otherwise he would have never made it through the traps."

"So, there's no-one around here that has the ability to see inside mechanical things?"

Gurpreet shook his head. "We haven't had anyone with that ability here since your dad. It would have been nice to have someone around with that ability, but it hasn't been essential. We could have brought someone in if we needed, but it isn't all that important that we retrieve the Impression Stone so don't worry if you can't get it."

Adam pondered the information for a moment, until Gurpreet interrupted.

"I'm heading to the game now. When you get stuck or frustrated walk over to the ball diamond and watch the game."

It's tough to get stuck when you don't know where to start, though Adam as he nodded to Gurpreet.

Gurpreet made his way back to the van as Adam started looking at the statue a lot closer. Brutus was a few feet in the air on top of a platform and was built roughly the same size as a normal person. One hand was in the air in a sort of waving position, while the other was held lower as if it were grabbing something.

Adam heard the van leave as he investigated, but it only registered somewhere far off in his mind as he had become so interested in the statue. He decided to start at the bottom and work his way up – which meant investigating the pedestal first.

The pedestal seemed to be made of some sort of metal like the statue; although he was sure it wasn't bronze. Looking around, nothing stood out in particular. The only thing different on the entire pedestal was the plaque, so he stopped and read.

"Brutus Killaly – 1872 – 1949. Brutus Killaly founded the town bearing his name on this spot in 1915. Besides being an adventurer, explorer, and master builder, his love of music, dance and good times will be forever remembered."

Adam inspected the plaque closer, but saw nothing unusual. He tried to wiggle it and pry it, but it held firm.

"Hey, what do you think you're doing," Adam heard someone yell from somewhere behind. He turned and saw a boy a little older than himself jogging in his direction.

The boy had shaggy sandy hair and looked intimidating, especially due to his size. His jog was heavy and sloppy. Just then, Adam realized that it must have looked like he was trying to wreck the statue. He pushed his brain to figure out a reason to tell the approaching boy before he got himself hurt or in trouble.

Adam decided to try the diplomatic approach. "Hi." He said as the other boy stopped next to him. "I'm just trying to figure something out."

The boy eyed him suspiciously, but said nothing.

"...uh...I heard that this statue holds a secret. I don't want to wreck it." Adam continued, nervous.

The boy continued eyeing him with suspicion. "Yeah, we've all heard that rumour too," he finally said after a long silence.

Adam was surprised to hear that. The boy wasn't that much older than he was, so he couldn't be part of the League yet since Grayson was the only town where children knew the secret.

"Every once in a while we see someone here trying to pry off the plaque or move his arms. I think it's just a rumour, though – an old ghost story. The statue isn't that old."

"I'm Adam McTaggart from Grayson," said Adam, extending his hand for a handshake.

The look of suspicion on the boy's face slowly faded a little. "Oh, so you came with the ball team and figured you'd take a look while you were here."

Adam nodded.

The boy took Adam's hand and gave it a quick shake. "I'm Derek Gunderson. My dad's the Mayor."

Adam nodded and looked back to the statue. "So lots of people have tried to figure this out?" he asked.

Derek nodded. "In the last year we've had a lot of people stop and look at it. All we've heard is that it holds a secret – but nothing else. No clues or anything. My dad asked me to keep an eye on it so no one wrecks it."

Adam didn't like hearing that. If a bunch of other people had already tried and failed, how could he think he would succeed?

He looked at Derek. "Do you mind if I keep trying? I promise I don't want to damage anything."

Derek gazed at Adam as if he were trying to read Adam's mind, then nodded.

Adam turned back to the statue and thought for a moment. The secret had to have something to do with his new-found ability, so he placed his hands on two sides of the pedestal and concentrated. Nothing happened, so he tried the other two sides, then alternate sides. Still nothing happened.

Derek was standing there watching him with a smirk on his face. Adam realized that it probably looked funny that this strange boy was hugging the pedestal in order to reach opposite sides. "Never seen anyone try that before," he said.

Adam stepped away from the statue to get a better look. He thought hard and remembered the previous year when Elianora told him to find Brutus. Well, he found Brutus. And Brutus was a big bronze statue, standing in a funny position. Everyone kept telling him he needed to talk to Brutus to get the Impression Stone.

A thought dawned on Adam. He looked at the pedestal and noticed that there was just enough space for someone to stand on top of it with the statue, so he climbed up. Derek seemed interested in what Adam was doing and moved in closer to watch.

Once he was up, he examined the face of the statue. The craftsmanship was amazing, but he could see a fine line around the mouth and jaw if he looked really close. The jaw might possibly open up if you knew how to unlock it. Adam grabbed the chin and tried moving it in different directions with no luck.

"I've seen guys do that before too," said Derek. "Didn't work for them either."

Adam had another thought. He placed his hands on either side of the statue's head and tried to see inside. He closed his eyes and pulled the statue to him as hard as he could, but it didn't work.

"That one's new," said Derek.

He's getting really annoying, thought Adam.

As he held the head in his hands, he decided to actually talk to Brutus. "Open up," he said.

Again, nothing happened.

Frustrated, he climbed back down from the pedestal and took a few steps backwards to get a better look at the statue.

"Don't feel bad, I've seen a lot of guys try a lot of things and nothing has worked so far," said Derek.

Adam looked at the statue one more time and thought about the words on the plaque. That's when a thought hit him. Why was Brutus standing in that position?

Again Adam climbed onto the pedestal. He already realized that he was going to look really strange in a moment, but he was willing to try anything. He moved into position and put one hand in the hand of the statue that was raised, then one hand around its back. The other hand of the statue rested on Adam's hip.

Derek laughed at the sight. "Wow, now I've seen everything."

Adam ignored Derek as much as he could, although he could feel Derek watching him and laughing. He shook it off and tried to concentrate, but found it difficult as his mind kept playing pictures of how funny he must have looked.

He breathed deeply and pushed all other thoughts aside except for trying to see into the statue. In the next moment, he was inside the statue looking around.

He was inside a small room with no windows, but he could see just fine. Again, there was no source of light that he could pinpoint but the walls shone the color of new bronze. If he had been claustrophobic at all, that place would have sent him into a fit of panic.

As he looked around he saw something on the wall straight ahead. When he approached, it became clear what it was. Instructions were carved into the bronze on the wall. He studied the instructions for a moment before he brought himself back out of the statue again.

Remembering the instructions, Adam kept holding the raised hand of the statue, stood on both of its feet, reached around it in a big bear hug and laid his head into the crook of its neck.

He could hear Derek laughing at the strange sight, but he didn't care. He pulled hard on the hand that was in the air and heard a small pop next to his ear. He leaned back and saw that Brutus's mouth had popped open. Inside his mouth was a small pebble.

It was the Impression Stone.

CHAPTER SEVEN

Adam grabbed the Impression Stone and closed Brutus's mouth again before hopping down from the pedestal. He was surprised and happy that he was able to figure it out, until he noticed Derek staring at him with his mouth hanging open.

"How'd you do that?" asked Derek.

Adam shrugged.

"What was in there?"

Adam wasn't sure what to say, but in the position he was in, he had to tell Derek something.

"Just a pebble. It's a keepsake of a really old lady from Grayson. That's why we've all been here trying to find it. It means a lot to her."

Derek squinted. He didn't seem to believe Adam.

"Can I see it?" he asked.

Adam shrugged, not sure if he should, but decided he wasn't in a position to refuse. He held it out for Derek to see.

Derek snatched it from Adam's hand and held it in the air.

"Don't drop it!" said Adam, nervously wondering what Derek was going to do next.

Derek turned the stone in his fingers, inspecting it as it moved. "This is all that was in there?" he asked.

Adam nodded.

Derek looked back to the pebble for a few more moments. It was the same size as the first Impression Stone Adam had seen, but this one was shaped different and had one sharp side.

"Well, I know you say that it belongs to someone from Grayson, but it's been here in Killaly for years, hidden in a statue of its founder. I don't think I can let you keep this," he said.

Adam's heart sank. Derek was much bigger than him, so Adam wouldn't be able to take it back by force. Maybe if he could get to Gurpreet, Gurpreet could talk some sense into Derek.

"But, I don't want to be accused of stealing this from you, so let's go talk to my dad about it. He'll know what to do. Come on."

Derek waved for Adam to follow and walked up the street toward the middle of town. Adam followed without question, thinking this was probably the only way he *might* get the Impression Stone back, but not holding much hope. Chances were that Derek's father thought just like his son.

They walked up the block and turned the corner, away from the direction of the ball diamonds. Half a block later they were standing at the front door of a large newer house. Derek motioned for Adam to stay put as he opened the door and yelled, "Dad. Come out here."

A few moments later, a voice boomed from somewhere inside. "What do you need Derek?"

"Just come outside," Derek replied.

Thirty seconds later the door swung open and out stepped a larger older version of Derek. His face was expressionless until he saw Adam, and then it broke into the wide smile of a politician.

"Hello," said the man, "I'm John Gunderson, Mayor of Killaly." He put out his hand to shake Adam's.

Adam took it and shook back.

"Dad," Derek interrupted before Adam could speak, "He opened the statue!"

John looked surprised. "What do you mean 'opened' the statue?"

"He did something to it and the mouth popped open. This was inside." Derek handed the Impression Stone to his dad.

John looked from the stone to Adam and back to the stone, his face expressionless as he seemed deep in thought.

"He's from Grayson and says it belongs to an old lady that lives there, but I figure it belongs to Killaly."

John looked at Adam again. "Who does it 'belong' to in Grayson?" he asked.

"Elianora White, sir," Adam replied.

John's face remained expressionless, and he stayed silent for a few more seconds. Adam didn't know what to think as he waited, hoping that John knew who Elianora was.

John began to nod slightly, "Well, they don't get any older than her now, do they?" he said. "What's your name, son?"

"Adam McTaggart."

John's face changed at the mention of his name. "Ed's son?" he asked.

Adam nodded.

John smiled slightly as he stared at Adam. "I should have seen the resemblance. You look just like him – and your Grandpa. You know your grandpa was the Mayor of Killaly at one time?"

Adam nodded. "Yeah. I just found that out."

"Now I understand why you were able to figure out the secret of the statue. Family secret probably, handed down. You don't have to say anything – I understand."

Adam decided it was best not to say any more and just shrugged his shoulders.

"I *am* surprised that it is only this little rock that was in there. The way people were coming out of Grayson to look at the statue I would have expected a pile of gold or at least a few diamonds to pop out."

"Who did you see looking at the statue?" asked Adam, curious.

"Well, Gurpreet was here a few times – everyone knows him. Then there was your Mayor, Jeff."

Adam made a face and John picked up on it right away.

"Sorry," said Adam.

"Don't worry; we won't judge Grayson by its Mayor."

Adam smiled a little. "Anyone else?" he asked again.

Derek offered up the next couple of people. "The guy that owns the meat shop, and that really fat guy that sells insurance," he said.

"Karl Klein?" asked Adam.

Derek and John nodded.

"Yeah," Derek continued, "I've watched him quite a few times. He never does anything, just stands and stares at Brutus. It's pretty creepy."

"Derek, this does indeed belong to Elianora White. We'll be giving it back to her," said John.

Derek nodded, but his face showed his disappointment.

"I need to speak to Adam about some boring things. Can you go to the ball diamond and tell Gurpreet to pick Adam up here after the game?"

Derek paused for a moment, thinking of some reason to stay, but gave up shortly. He turned and started walking slowly in the direction of the diamonds.

"Come in," said John. "Just leave your shoes on."

Adam followed John into the house. They walked to the back of the long building and into John's office. The house was large and clean, yet filled with electronics, paintings and general stuff. John's office was much the same, except all of the mementos seemed to be personal to him. Behind his desk and higher up the wall was a lion's head mounted as a trophy.

"As you can appreciate, Derek knows nothing of the League yet. We aren't quite as lucky as Grayson that we can tell everyone," he said, sounding bitter.

Adam nodded slowly, unsure what John was getting at exactly, and he couldn't help but stare at the lion's head. John picked up on it.

"I shot that in Africa a few years back. Beautiful animal. So powerful."

Adam continued to stare at the lion as he nodded.

"So, you're the famous Mctaggart that outsmarted Larix," he continued after a pause.

The word famous tore Adam away from the lion and stuck in his head for a moment. *What did he mean by* 'famous'.

"I didn't outsmart him," Adam replied. "I just got lucky."

John nodded, smiling again. "That's what I had assumed," he said. "In all of the stories of people going against his wishes, very few have ever survived to talk about it. If they did survive they usually had a Teneo at their side."

Adam had never heard any other stories of encounters with Larix, even in the class at school. He didn't know how to respond, so he just sat there.

A few awkward moments of silence later, John continued.

"What was he like?" he asked. "I've heard stories about him all of my life and always wondered what it would be like to meet him. He's such a great strategist. You'll learn that in time. I may not like the things he's done, but I admire his strategy. You see, Politics is much like war, you have groups fighting for what they believe, and in the end it's either the strongest or the smartest one that wins. These days you can't just go around and kill your opponent, at least in Western civilization anyway, so you have to outsmart your enemy."

Adam nodded in agreement, although he was feeling apprehensive. John sounded as if he *wanted* to meet Larix.

John seemed to sense that. He cleared his throat and his mood seemed to lighten. "Of course, I would only want to meet him if he was locked in a very secure jail cell and I could ask him questions about strategy. He's much too dangerous to meet any other way, as you already know."

Adam didn't believe him at all. The words were sincere, but didn't feel genuine.

"So?" asked John.

Adam stared back at him, wondering what he wanted to hear. After a few moments, he cleared his throat. "Well, I don't know what to say, other than he's pretty full of himself."

John nodded, "Yes, his boasting is legendary. Even your Mayor doesn't compare."

Adam nodded in agreement as he remembered thinking about that similarity while he was in the caves helping Larix get past the traps. John was right about that.

"And he has no concern for regular people at all," Adam continued.

"With the number of people he's killed over the centuries, that's a pretty well known fact," said John.

"Yeah, but when you hear him you understand just how little he cares. It's like he's bored with killing people already – like a spoiled kid gets bored with a toy," said Adam, "and he was having a tantrum because someone took his favourite one."

"Well, that's true, isn't it?" said John. "We all know the story of the Heartstone, but none of us would have believed it was in Grayson all of these years."

"But it wasn't," replied Adam. "Someone took it and now no-one knows where it is. As far as Elianora knows, it could have been gone for a decade already."

John eyed Adam closely, like a poker player looking for a tell in his opponent. Adam had the feeling that John was pretty good at reading people. When a few seconds had passed, Adam could feel the intensity of his gaze lighten as if he were convinced that Adam was being truthful.

"You're a lot like your Grandpa, kid," he said. "He was tough to read too. You know that a lot of people think you smuggled the Heartstone out from under Larix's nose. Me – well, I think you're telling the truth that it was just a fake you found, which leads to the question of where it is now."

Adam shrugged, "If I would have had it when I got out of the caverns, it would have exploded because Elianora was there."

John shook his head, "Don't forget that Larix was right next to you. His presence could have kept it from exploding again. He's been around Teneo in the past and been able to keep it under control."

Adam hadn't heard any of those stories, but now he understood how people could suspect him.

Silence slipped in and sucked life from the room again. Adam thought about some of the things John had told him when he remembered a question he wanted to ask.

"Mr. Gunderson,"

"Please, call me John," he smiled his most political smile.

"Uh, John...what can you tell me about my Grandpa? I didn't know him at all."

"Your grandpa was a strict, hard working man. That trait made him difficult to work with, but he was always straight forward. Maybe he was a bit too strict, and that's why your dad never came back after he left for training with the League. Just like your grandpa, your dad wasn't lazy, but he was a lot more relaxed when he dealt with issues. Your grandpa was more like an army drill sergeant. Don't get me wrong, I learned a lot from both of them - but it's hard to believe they were father and son."

John paused as he looked at Adam.

"And then there's you. I'm not sure just what to think about you yet. I'll bet you fall somewhere in the middle. You show up here out of the blue and open that statue in matter of minutes when other men have spent a lot of time thinking about it and trying different things. You must have known something that the rest didn't."

Adam didn't feel like telling John about his ability to see into objects, so he played along. "Yep, family secret," he replied. That seemed to satisfy John.

"Do you know why Elianora wants this particular stone back?" he asked.

Adam shrugged. "She told me they are really rare and she might be able to use it again."

John stared at Adam. "Don't be that naïve, son. Yeah, that stone's pretty rare, but she wants to see what information is stored on it. See if what's on it was changed at all."

Adam was surprised. John noticed and continued. "Like I said before about politics, I like to stay informed. Good strategy comes from good information. Knowledge is power. It pays to stay well connected."

The look on John's face told Adam that this particular information probably wasn't supposed to be shared with John but he had found a way to hear it anyway.

"The League, for all of its secrets, is still made up of people – and people like to talk, especially when they know a secret," he continued. "But don't worry; unlike a lot of people, I can keep a secret. I'll find out what's on that Impression Stone eventually. That's why I am letting you take it back to her. Besides, no one in Killaly can connect with it enough to read it anyway."

Thoughts raced through Adam's mind as he tried to figure out how John was receiving his information. Someone in Grayson was obviously feeding it to him, but who?

A door opened somewhere in the house and closed again.

"Derek must be back," said John, but the sound of multiple footsteps echoed down the hall.

The office door opened and Derek stepped in, followed close behind by Gurpreet. Adam had known Gurpreet long enough to see the concern in his face, although he was hiding it well. He approached John and held out his hand.

"Hello John, good to see you," he said, shaking hands.

"And you too," said John in reply. "Did our team beat you that quickly? The game shouldn't be over yet."

Gurpreet smiled a fake smile, "No, it's tie game right now actually because we are down a couple of key players. Once Derek told me that Adam was here I figured I should bring him to the game to watch the rest."

John smiled an equally fake smile. "Good idea. What did Derek tell you so far?"

"Only that he found Adam at the statue and brought him to see you," replied Gurpreet.

John nodded and looked at his son. "Good job," he told Derek, then turned back to Gurpreet, "Well, it looks like you only needed to know a McTaggart family secret to open the statue."

Gurpreet looked at Adam, his face calm and cool. "I thought he might be able to figure it out. He's pretty clever you know."

John nodded. "I figured that out from our short conversation." He looked at Adam, "It was great speaking with you. If you ever want to chat again, I am always available. If you want to see any more of the game, though, I had better not keep you."

Adam felt strange about the conversation he had just witnessed. The word spoken didn't go together with the feeling he had in his gut that there was much more said behind the words. He never thought he was able to pick up on those type of things, but maybe he was learning how as he got older.

"Yes, we should go. Thanks for your hospitality," said Gurpreet.

Adam felt a tap on his shoulder a moment later. It shook him out of his thoughts. "Uh...yeah...thanks," he managed to spit out.

"Derek, please show our guests to the door," said John and they followed Derek out.

As they walked fast toward the baseball diamond, Adam asked, "What was that all about? I heard you talking, but none of the words matched the meaning."

Gurpreet kept looking toward their destination, but Adam could tell that his question had interrupted Gurpreet's thoughts.

"You have the Impression Stone?"

Adam felt in his pocket and nodded.

"Good. Hang on to it until later – and keep it safe."

"Are you going to tell me anything?" Adam asked again.

"Sorry, just got lost in thought," Gurpreet answered as he slowed from a fast to a regular walk, "I just wanted to get away from the house first. John and I have known each other for some time now, and sadly he doesn't like me or anyone from Grayson much."

"Why?" asked Adam.

"Well, he doesn't like me because I was chosen as Number 2 instead of him."

"That would do it," said Adam. "He seems pretty power-hungry."

Gurpreet nodded. "You got that out of your short conversation?"

"He basically told me that all he cares about is power in the first few minutes."

Gurpreet chuckled. "Yep. And he wonders why he wasn't picked. Anyway, he has been very critical of Grayson for the way we handled the Heartstone, not even realizing it was gone. He even called for me to resign or be replaced."

"He probably nominated himself to replace you," said Adam.

Gurpreet smiled in response. "We can talk more later. Let's get back to the game," he said as they could see the ball diamond getting close.

When they arrived, the news wasn't good. One of the Killaly team had hit a home run with two players on base, leaving Grayson down by three.

By the end of the game, Grayson managed to get only one more run and it wasn't nearly enough for the win. Adam and Mark had sat in the bleachers for the remainder of the game. Mark had looked up from his portable video game when Adam sat down, and Adam had the impression that Mark hadn't even noticed that his dad had been gone.

The players all shook hands and returned to their benches, packing up their things and heading to their cars. Soon, Adam and the Gupta's were seated in the van again and on their way back to Grayson.

CHAPTER EIGHT

As they drove, Adam told them all that had happened since he was left with Brutus. Mark even listened to the whole story before putting his headphones back on.

Gurpreet drove quietly for a while before speaking again.

"Will your mom be angry if you're out for another hour or so?" he asked.

Adam shook his head. He knew Mary was out for the evening, and he also had a pretty good idea where they would be going.

Gurpreet smiled. "Ok then. We'll drop Mark off at home and continue on."

"Wait, what?" said Mark from the back seat, obviously having caught the last part of the conversation.

"You're going home while we continue on," Gurpreet replied.

"Aww, why?" Mark whined. "It's summer holidays. I don't have to go to sleep yet. It's still *early*."

"We're just going to see Elianora and give her the stone. Adam will probably have to tell the whole story over again," said Gurpreet, confirming Adam's suspicion.

Mark thought about it for a few seconds. Adam knew that it was a struggle between hearing the discussion with Elianora and being somewhere with electricity, but because Gurpreet had played it down, Adam knew the answer before Mark spoke again.

"Oh, ok. Just drop me off."

Adam smiled. He knew Mark well.

The van hummed along the highway carrying its silent occupants onward. Adam felt his pocket, making sure he hadn't lost the stone. It felt the same size as the other Impression Stone he had held last year, but something was different. It wasn't the same shape as the other one, and he felt the sharp side he had seen when Derek was examining it.

After a couple of turns, the van slowed to a stop outside of the Gupta's house. Mark hopped out, turned and gave a short wave meaning 'see ya', and then headed for the house. The van pulled away as soon as Mark had swung the house door open.

"She's going to be pretty happy that you were able to open the statue. We didn't want to have to break it open. John would dislike me even more if we had to destroy their statue," said Gurpreet.

Adam agreed. From what he had learned about John, dislike was a pretty weak description.

In a matter of minutes the van was pulling into the long, nearly overgrown driveway once again. Gurpreet grimaced as he heard the branches scrape the sides, especially since it was a nearly new vehicle.

Adam followed Gurpreet up to the porch door, standing behind him as he knocked. After hearing the customary welcome, a light appeared in the porch. The familiar blue-green glow of the Lumiens streamed from behind the door as Gurpreet pulled it open. Stepping inside, they found Elianora in her living room, this time knitting a slipper. The first one of the pair was already finished, and it looked as if she had used every color she could find in the process. She looked up at them as they walked in, noticing the look on Adam's face as he stared at the slippers.

"I can knit you a pair as soon as I'm done with this one," she said with a smile.

Adam was caught off guard and didn't know how to reply. All he managed to get out was a grunt that sounded like, "Uh."

Elianora laughed. "I'm just kidding. I know they're ugly. I'm making them for Karl. He mentioned that he keeps losing his and hinted that if he could only find a pair that had a lot of strong colors, he wouldn't lose them anymore. It's a surprise, so I'd appreciate it if you wouldn't say anything."

Adam was relieved. He hadn't gotten used to her sense of humour completely in the time he had spent with her so far. Gurpreet seemed to have known she was teasing because he had a wide smile on his face when Adam looked over at him.

"I take it that you were able to open the statue, otherwise you wouldn't be here," she stated matter of fact.

Adam reached into his pocket and handed the stone over. Elianora took it gently and looked at it for a moment before picking up a box from the table next to her. It looked like a little wooden jewellery box, and it was engraved with intricate pictures and words that Adam didn't understand. She opened the lid and placed the impression stone inside before turning back to look at Adam.

"Thank you for figuring out the statue. I thought you would be the one to open it."

Adam was hoping to watch her connect with the stone before he left, but knew she would want to hear everything that had happened.

"Don't you want to connect with the stone and see if it changed?" he asked.

"I already did," she replied.

Adam gave her a confused look.

"As soon as I touched it I saw everything it holds," she said, understanding his confusion. "I only need to touch an object to connect with it, unlike most people. I've been doing this for a long time, though."

Adam was amazed that she was able to connect and read everything in that short of a time. She looked so young that it was hard to remember how old she was, even though he still didn't know exactly how old.

"...and it's exactly as I thought it would be, in case you are wondering." She finished as if she were able to read his mind.

"The only issue he had was that Derek Gunderson caught him at the statue and forced him to talk to John," said Gurpreet.

Elianora shrugged and frowned. "Unfortunate, but not unexpected. They've been keeping a pretty good eye on it for the last year – and for that I am glad. Do you have time to tell me everything that happened?"

Adam agreed and began at the point just before Gurpreet 'introduced' him to Brutus.

"You guys," Elianora shook her finger at Gurpreet.

Gurpreet smiled a mischievous smile.

"You would have done the same thing to me if I hadn't been suspicious that Brutus had the Heartstone."

Gurpreet nodded. "Probably."

Elianora smiled, shook her head and turned to Adam. "Go on."

Adam finished telling her the story and decided to ask one of the many questions on his mind.

"I don't get it. You had no idea about Brutus?" he asked.

Elianora shook her head. "I tasked your Grandfather with hiding the second Impression Stone in a way that Larix wouldn't be able to figure out. I asked him not to tell me how it was hidden either, but to give me a clue. His clue ended up being 'talk to Brutus', that's all. Of course, I had no idea what he meant, so that was perfect. When he had finished, we wiped his memory. The problem was that a while after we found out the Heartstone was missing from the Radome caves, I had a suspicion it might have been hidden with Brutus so I had some of the Senior members try and get it. I wasn't exactly excited to go there myself and find it in case it really was there." She made the noise and motions with her hands to indicate an explosion.

"Why have two Impression Stones?" asked Adam.

"I always like to have a backup plan. No plan is completely foolproof, but we try and do the best we can. Even though we want to make it difficult for Larix to get the Heartstone back, we don't want to make it impossible for anyone to transfer it to another location. Moving it around a lot has seemed to work best for us in the past. Two stones gives us two options."

There were so many questions that Adam had wanted to ask but he couldn't put them into words fast enough.

"We should get back to town now", said Gurpreet, "It's getting late." His words interrupted Adam's thoughts and all Adam could do was nod before being shuffled toward the door.

The ride back to town was quiet. Adam wished he would have asked more questions about his family, or what was the deal with Killaly – especially John Gunderson.

"I forgot to tell Elianora about John. I think someone here is feeding him information," Adam blurted out.

Gurpreet raised his eyebrows. "Like what?"

"He knew you were trying to get an Impression Stone out of Brutus, and the way he said it sounded like it was top secret."

Gurpreet chuckled. "That's John for you. We told him exactly what we were looking for when we asked him to keep an eye on Brutus. He was just testing you."

Adam said, "Ok," but still felt like John was hiding something else.

As they stopped in front of Adam's house, Gurpreet spoke. "Thanks for getting that stone tonight. I know Ellie appreciates it a lot more than she let on."

"Glad I could help," he replied as he stepped out of the car. "Thanks for taking me."

Gurpreet waved in return while Adam closed the van door. Adam waved back as Gurpreet pulled away, and then he turned toward his house. He hadn't realized until that point just how tired the evening's events had made him.

It was a really dark night and there were no lights on inside or outside of the house. Mary would never leave any on so the power bill would stay low. The only problem was that on dark nights there was so little moonlight Adam couldn't put the key in the keyhole. The nearest street light was further down the block and obstructed by a large tree.

Adam took the key from its hiding spot under the side of the step and went to open the door. To his surprise, it was unlocked. He wondered if Mary hadn't gone out for the evening after all because she usually locked the door behind her if Adam wasn't home. As soon as he turned on the light, though, he knew she wasn't there.

While they were out, the house had been broken into.

CHAPTER NINE

Adam stared in shock at the sight. The cupboard doors in the kitchen were open with the contents scattered all over the counter top. The lower cupboards had been emptied onto the floor. He looked over at the living room and the cushions were pulled off of the two chairs. Everything on the mantle had been gone through and moved around.

After a few seconds standing still surveying the mess, it occurred to Adam that nothing seemed to be missing. Whoever broke in must have been looking for something specific. That's when it occurred to him.

He felt his pockets and the pin was still there, since he had taken it to Killaly just-in-case. As fast as he could, he turned and bolted outside to his garage. He slammed the door open and flipped on the light, but barely registered the fact that tools and parts were lying everywhere. His eyes were fixed on the back corner where a furnace would have once been. That was the spot where his best hiding spot was, and where he kept the little amount of money he had.

The tin heat shields that kept the walls from burning had provided a place for Adam hide items he didn't want

Mary to know about, but they were ripped away from the wall.

Adam ran to the corner to survey the damage. His money was still there, and so was the envelope full of pictures related to the Sentinel League. He quickly thumbed through them but didn't notice anything missing.

Adam quickly reattached the heat shields to the wall again, thinking about the break-in the entire time. By the time he had finished, he was fairly certain that someone was either looking for his dad's lapel pin or the Heartstone, but exactly who was another question. He had been extremely clear that the Heartstone he had found in the cave was a fake the previous summer, and all of the upper members of the League seemed to believe him.

That's when the thought hit him. Maybe Larix was back. He was the only person Adam could think of that thought Adam had the real Heartstone. The thought made him shudder, but he pushed the thought away when he remembered Elianora saying Larix was confirmed to be in South Africa the day before.

After looking around some more, Adam decided he would finish cleaning his garage later and check out more of the house. Maybe he could get everything cleaned up before Mary got home. He was sure she would blame him for it anyway, even if she had been in a good mood earlier. She had been so happy to go to the dinner theater with Mrs. Garagan that Adam worried Mary would never leave the house again if she found out.

Back in the house, Adam checked his room, and it was in the same condition as the kitchen. He could close the door and leave it for later too, so he moved on to start in Mary's room. When he opened the door, again he was surprised. It hadn't been touched.

Why would someone rip apart the whole house and not her room, he wondered.

He closed the door again and returned to the main floor to start cleaning. Thoughts ran through his head as he worked. Why didn't they go through Mary's room? Had they left it intentionally or did they get interrupted? Or did they know how long Adam and Mary would be gone and run out of time?

The cleaning went fast, mostly because whoever went through the house had pulled everything apart neatly, so it was only a matter of putting things back where they belonged. The fact that the McTaggarts didn't own much also helped. Within half an hour he was done the rest of the house and started working in his room.

As he finished re-folding his clothes and putting them on the bed he heard a car pull up outside, the door close and then the house door opening. He ran down the stairs to see if Mary noticed anything was wrong with the house. When he reached the bottom step, he realized that he had *run* down the stairs instead of tiptoeing quietly and thought he would be scolded for being so loud.

Instead, Mary was smiling. Adam was happy to see it, and it confirmed the fact that he didn't want to tell Mary about the break in.

"Oh, you're home," she said as she glanced at the clock. It was 11:35.

Adam nodded. He suppressed the urge to say "obviously," and instead said, "How was the dinner theater? Looks like you had fun."

Mary nodded in return as she hung up her jacket. "It was ok, I guess. Not as good as I expected, but worth going to see."

She looked around as if she sensed that something was different.

Adam came up with a story quick. "I dusted everything when I got home. Just felt like doing it before I went to bed." He wasn't really lying as he *had* wiped down the surfaces as he straightened up, since everything was out of place anyway.

Mary accepted his explanation easily. "I'm going to bed. I'm really tired. Mr. Garagan gave me the morning off tomorrow so I'm going to sleep in. Don't stay up too late and keep the volume down if you watch TV."

Adam had heard this sentence a million times before, and simply replied, "Ok."

Mary made her way upstairs while Adam breathed a sigh of relief, seeming to have covered up all that had happened. His relaxation was short lived when a cry came from the top of the stairs.

"What happened in here?" came Mary's voice, and it sounded upset.

Adam was jolted into action, running up the stairs while trying to remember what he had missed cleaning. As he reached the top, he realized that he hadn't closed his bedroom door and Mary had seen everything scattered about. He was never allowed to let his room get that messy, and he knew it.

Mary turned from the bedroom back to Adam, but she didn't look as angry as Adam had expected. As she stared at him, he came up with an explanation.

"I was just cleaning that up," he managed to spit out, wondering how she was going to react to the fact that they had someone go through their house. Maybe she would just think someone went through his room and nowhere else

Her face softened. "Well, you must be in a cleaning mood tonight. You didn't have to pull everything out of your dresser and off your shelves, though. It would have been easier to do them one at a time."

Adam looked at his room. Yes, everything was out of the drawers and off the shelves, but it hadn't been thrown around like you would assume. Everything was stacked somewhat neatly, although in no particular order. It dawned on Adam that Mary thought this was how he was sorting and cleaning his room.

"Oh...well...uh, one thing just led to another, you know, and I was just starting to put things back again."

Mary smiled. "Don't stay up too late. You can finish it tomorrow."

Adam was stunned but tried not to show it, so he said, "Ok...goodnight."

Mary managed a quick "night" before heading into her room. Adam closed the door, flopped on his bed and breathed deeply. He felt bad that he hadn't told his mom what had really happened, but at the same time he had managed not to outright lie to her - just forgot to give her the details.

Soon the excitement of the day caught up with him, and before he knew it he had fallen asleep, fully clothed. When he woke the next morning, he had barely moved the entire night since everything that had been stacked on his bed was still there and not toppled onto the floor.

After carefully getting off his bed so he didn't disturb anything, he set to work putting everything back in its place. It had been a dreamless night and he was still waking up as he cleaned.

The only drawer that hadn't been emptied was his top dresser drawer - the one filled with parts and components he had collected and used to build things. It had been rifled through, but everything still seemed to be there.

By the time he had finished, he wandered downstairs, ate a quick breakfast and headed outside to his garage. He glanced at the clock on his way out and couldn't believe it was only just past 7:30 am. He felt like he had slept for a lot longer.

Until he opened the door, he had almost forgotten that his garage was still a mess. As he stepped inside, he surveyed the interior and realized that whoever had gone through everything had done it in the same way as the rest of the house. Except for the tin that was pulled from the wall the previous night, everything was stacked somewhat neatly all around. The good thing was that it wouldn't take long to clean.

As he worked his mind ran through scenarios, everything from Larix returning to a random hitchhiker looking for food, and each scenario got more and more unlikely. Larix was known to be in South Africa at the moment, he remembered, so that wasn't a possibility, and Grayson was so far from anywhere that there were never hitchhikers in town. If there were it would be the biggest news of the week.

Soon everything was back to the way Adam had it before, so he sat in his chair and put his feet on the table, thinking about the day ahead. He was pretty sure he was going to tell Gurpreet about the break in as soon as he could, maybe they would even go tell Elianora together.

Adam looked at his watch. It still wasn't even 9am. Mary wouldn't be up yet, so he didn't want to go in the house in case he disturbed her. Kevin would be up and working on the farm most likely, because if he wasn't working he would have been there to see Adam already. Jimmy and Mark would still be asleep, since neither one seemed to get out of bed much before lunch, and Adam didn't feel like seeing Gurpreet quite yet. He decided to wait until after lunch before trying to find anyone.

After looking through the small stack of salvaged, cover-less comics that he had read a thousand times, he decided to practice seeing again. He had already seen inside the antique transistor radio, so he looked around to find something else he might have missed that might work. There wasn't much selection though, as he had already ripped apart everything else just to find out how it worked.

As he searched, he heard faint footsteps on the sidewalk getting closer. It was probably just someone out for a walk that morning, so he ignored the sound and kept looking. As soon as he heard the familiar crunch of gravel, he knew he someone was coming up their driveway, but he didn't recognize the footsteps. They sounded heavy, but not in the same way as Mark's. The person was approaching at a normal pace, and although Adam thought the footsteps sounded familiar, he couldn't place them.

What if it's whoever broke in last night? he thought as the footsteps didn't stop at the house. The person was heading straight to the garage.

He froze where he stood and listened until the person knocked on the garage door. The sharp sound made Adam jump as he wasn't expecting it, even though he knew he should have.

"Hello," sounded a gruff voice from the other side of the door.

The voice shocked Adam almost as much as the knock.

It was the voice of Ben Casey.

CHAPTER TEN

Since the events of the previous summer, Adam hadn't seen much of Ben Casey other than riding past on his bike while Ben worked in his yard. Each time Ben would glare at Adam with suspicion and Adam always felt as if he were under interrogation from a distance.

But why was Ben standing outside his door and how did he know to find Adam in the garage? Adam wondered.

Ben hadn't even tried the house first. It was like he knew where Adam was.

Adam cleared his throat and managed to say, "Just a second," before he made his way to the door and opened it.

"Mr. Casey...hi...Why are *you* here?" Adam realized as he said the words that they sounded a lot more harsh than he had intended.

Ben glared at him for a second before saying, "Aren't we just a little ray of sunshine this morning? I think that's what I'll call you from now on - Sunshine."

Adam felt sheepish. "Sorry. I didn't mean it like that," he said in an apologetic tone. "What can I do for you?"

Ben nodded, accepting his apology. "First, call me Ben. Mr. Casey reminds me of being in a courtroom a little too much."

Adam nodded but wondered why and how many times Ben had been in a courtroom.

"Second, I need your help," he continued. "I want to cut my lawn today, but my lawn mower won't start. I've heard you're pretty handy with these type of things. Think you could try and fix it?"

Adam was surprised that Ben was asking him for help.

"Sure, I can take a look," Adam replied.

"Can you come now? I want to get it done before lunch and nobody else can take a look until later today."

Adam then realized why Ben was asking him for help.

"Ok. You have tools, right?"

Ben nodded. "Should have everything you need."

"Let's go then," said Adam. Ben headed back down the gravel driveway and Adam followed as soon as he closed the garage door. He caught up to Ben soon after.

"You walked instead of driving?" asked Adam.

Ben gave a mean sounding chuckle. "You think I'm too old and fat to walk?" He replied with a straight face.

Adam couldn't tell if Ben was joking.

Ben managed to crack a slight smile. "It's a nice morning and I felt like a walk, that's all."

Adam didn't think he would ever get used to Ben's dry sense of humour. They walked a little further without speaking and Adam wondered if he should tell Ben about the break-in. Ben *was* the head of security after all. Everyone seemed to trust him in town, but Adam wasn't so sure. Yeah, Ben had saved Jimmy and Mark the previous year and taken out most of Larix's men by himself, but Adam still couldn't bring himself to trust Ben for some reason. Because of that, he kept his mouth shut. Instead, he figured he could kill some time by asking Ben about his problem.

"So what exactly is wrong with your mower," he asked.

"Won't start," Ben grunted in reply, then must have realized that Adam was helping him, so he continued. "I pulled the cord over and over and it doesn't even try to start. It has oil and gas in it."

That narrowed it down a little for Adam. The lawn mower he used at home was so old that he had learned a lot just keeping it running. Thankfully he had salvaged two other engines that weren't running but gave him enough parts to keep one of the three going.

"Did you pull out the spark plug and check it?" asked Adam.

Ben frowned. "Even though I *am* ruggedly handsome, I'm not terribly handy with those kind of things," he said, returning to grunting quietly as he walked.

Adam decided to ask no more and remained quiet until they arrived at Ben's shed a few minutes later.

The mower was sitting outside the shed on a small cement pad. Adam pulled the starter cord a few times and listened. It didn't sound like it was even close to starting, and there was a distinct smell of gasoline in the air.

"Do you have a spark plug wrench?" he asked Ben, "It doesn't seem to be sparking. I can smell the gas, so it's probably an ignition problem."

Ben looked at Adam as if Adam had just asked him a stupid question.

"Can't you just do that thing you do and *see* if it's got a spark?"

Adam wasn't completely surprised that Ben knew about Adam's ability already. Adam hadn't thought about using his ability to fix the mower but reasoned that Ben was probably right.

"uh, sure. I can give it a try," he said. "I'll go in and then get you to pull the cord a couple of times," he said, a little worry in his voice.

"I seen your dad do it on my old lawn mower a few times, so you got nothing to worry about," said Ben, reacting to Adam's hesitation.

Adam thought about it and bent down to the mower, placing his hands on both sides of the cylinder head while Ben moved into position. He closed his eyes for a second and when he opened them again, he found himself exactly where he wanted to be. He was standing inside the engine, next to the spark plug. Again, he could see everything clearly, although he couldn't see any source of light.

The electrode end of the spark plug rose out of the cylinder head next to him high enough that he realized that it was eye level. That's when he noticed that gravity didn't seem to matter either when he was inside an object. The spark plug he was standing beside was screwed into the top of the engine, but the engine was lying on its side. Where he was "standing" next to it, he should have fallen flat on his face.

Adam heard Ben clear his throat somewhere in the distance, and it reminded him of what he was there to do. He looked at the end of the spark plug and saw that it was really dirty and worn with a chunk of something stuck inside.

"Give it a pull," Adam yelled, thinking that he would need to be loud to be heard through the metal cylinder head.

"Quiet down, I can hear you fine," said Ben in an agitated reply. "Here goes."

Adam had a split second to be nervous before Ben yanked on the cord. It was scary to see the huge piston head race toward him and go back again over and over in a fraction of a second. He could see and smell the mist of fuel sucked in by the piston and shot out again when the exhaust valve opened, but there was no fire. Before Ben pulled again, Adam realized that he should probably watch the electrode for spark this time.

Ben yanked the cord again. Adam watched the electrode and there was nothing. Not even a hint of a spark. As soon as he saw that, he disconnected from the mower.

"I'm gonna need that spark plug wrench now," he said to Ben. "Your plug is fouled. Probably should be replaced. If that doesn't work, we'll try something else,"

Ben grunted and walked into his shed. Over Ben's shoulder, Adam could see part of the workbench that hid the entrance to the tunnels. It hadn't been apparent in his mind before how neat and orderly the tool shed had been the other times he had seen inside, but it only made sense after knowing how meticulous Ben was about the rest of his yard. It struck him differently seeing it at that moment.

Ben emerged holding the wrench. As he handed it to Adam, Adam noticed something he hadn't seen before. When Ben held out his hand to give Adam the tool, the tattoos on the underside of his forearm were visible. Adam had seen them before, but only now did he recognize the largest one. It was the Aeturnum symbol he had seen in the Heartstone.

Once Adam took the tool, Ben yanked his arm back. Adam hadn't realized that he was staring.

Feeling like he had been caught doing something wrong, he got to work on the spark plug right away. As soon as he had it out, he stood up and examined it, seeing that it looked exactly like it did when he was inside the engine only much smaller.

"Do you have a replacement?" he asked.

"Nope," Ben replied. "Gimme it and I'll go get one at the hardware store."

Adam handed it over, thoughts racing through his mind as it made connections. After seeing the Aeturnum tattoo and orderly manner of Ben's shed, Adam began to suspect that it was Ben who broke into his house due to the neat and tidy way everything had been gone through. But if Ben was part of Aeturnum, wouldn't he know where the Heartstone went? So what would he be looking for?

"You coming along?" asked Ben, sounding like he didn't want the company too much.

Adam shook his head as he thought of a quick excuse. "I'll just go see what Mark is up to for a few minutes," he replied.

Ben grunted. "Watch for when I get back," was all he said while pointing Adam out the driveway. Adam got the hint – Ben didn't want him there alone – so he walked casually across the street even though he was nearly bursting to tell Mark all that had happened.

Because he suspected Ben, he didn't want to tell Gurpreet about the break-in. He knew how much Gurpreet trusted Ben. In fact, all of the adults trusted

Ben, especially after the events of the last year. It would be hard, if not impossible to convince them otherwise.

Adam knocked on the door. A verbal squeal sounded from inside and little footsteps ran to the door before it opened a crack.

"Mark, it's for you," yelled one of the twins – Adam couldn't tell which one.

"Hi Adam," she continued.

"Hi," Adam replied. He couldn't tell if the girl speaking was Miri or Siri so he didn't even attempt to call her by her name. A second later the door opened wide and Mark pushed his way in front of the girl as if she wasn't even there. She let out a muffled "Hey," before walking away.

Mark yawned, still in his pyjamas. "Hey, what are you up to so early?" Mark stretched and groaned.

"It's not *that* early," replied Adam with a grin, and then remembered why he was there. "I'm just helping Ben fix his lawn mower. He went to the hardware store for parts and didn't want me to come along or stay at his place alone, so I came here. You have a minute to talk outside?" Adam jerked his head toward the driveway while giving Mark a look that said it was important.

For once, Mark was paying enough attention that he picked up on the gesture. "Uh, yeah. Let me just get some shoes."

Adam wandered out into the driveway where they would be out of earshot if they kept their voices down while still being able to see Ben approaching from a long way off when he returned. A few seconds later the door closed and Mark dragged his feet on the driveway as he walked over to Adam. He wore a pair of oversized slippers that made him drag his feet even more than usual.

On a normal day, Adam would have given his friend a hard time about his shoe choice, but other things were occupying his mind at the time. Adam quickly explained the events of the previous evening after being dropped off, but held his suspicion about Ben.

"Did you tell Ben? We have to tell Dad," said Mark.

"No," said Adam. "Not yet. There's more. I don't want to say right now. I want to talk it through with you guys before we do anything. Do you think you could find Jimmy and come to my place after lunch?"

Mark nodded. "Will do."

"I'll see if Kevin is able to come over too. Just wait in the garage if I'm not there," said Adam.

Mark nodded and then his eyes focused over Adam's shoulder. "There's Ben," he said.

"That was quick," said Adam. "See you later."

Mark shuffled back inside the house and Adam walked across the street to intercept Ben, waiting at the driveway until he arrived.

Ben handed him the spark plug as they continued toward the shed. Neither of them said anything and Adam installed the plug as soon as they reached the mower.

"Ready?" asked Adam.

Ben shrugged. "You gonna go in there again?" He pointed at the mower.

Adam hadn't thought about that. Being inside an engine when it starts didn't sound like a lot of fun. What if he got burned in there? Would it hurt his real body? Besides, he didn't exactly trust Ben. But Ben was about to say something to make sure that Adam tried.

"Your dad used to do it all the time. Said it was the best way to find problems," said Ben.

That was enough of a push for Adam. The thought that Ben could be lying to him went away at the mention of his dad and he nodded before placing his hands on the engine.

Ben moved into position and waited while Adam connected. Again he opened his eyes and found himself standing beside the spark plug, but this one was shiny and new. Nervously he said "Ready," and waited.

Time seemed to slow as he watched the piston get close then retract. The smell of gasoline filled his nose for a fraction of a second. The piston approached again and suddenly everything was fire and blinding light. It startled him so much that he let go of the engine and was torn back into his body again as he leaped backwards, landing on his side.

The mower purred in front of him, as much as a mower can purr anyway, and Ben cracked an odd smile. Adam wasn't sure if Ben was happy the mower was running or that Adam had been scared. He got up and brushed himself off while Ben stopped the engine.

"Thanks," said Ben in the gruff way only he seemed to be able to do, and he ruffled Adam's hair.

"No problem," replied Adam, feeling awkward about the gesture.

"I'm gonna cut my lawn now. You don't need me to hold your hand on the way home, do ya Sunshine?" said Ben.

Adam shook his head.

"Good," said Ben as he turned back to his mower.

Normally, Adam would have been a little upset at being treated the way Ben had just treated him, but because of everything on his mind, he was just happy to get away from there and back to his garage to think.

CHAPTER ELEVEN

It was almost 1:00 when Adam started riding toward Kevin's farm to see if Kevin could make it to the meeting. Adam wouldn't feel right if Kevin missed hearing about everything that had happened since they had seen each other last.

As soon as he passed the railroad tracks he saw Kevin pedaling out of his driveway, so he stopped and waited. Kevin saw him and took his hand off his handle bar just long enough for a quick wave.

Adam grinned. Somehow, Kevin always managed to make Adam a little happier.

"What's up?" asked Kevin as he stopped next to Adam.

"Lots," replied Adam.

Kevin's eyes widened before narrowing in an expression asking Adam to elaborate.

Adam shook his head. "I'll fill you in at the garage. Mark and Jimmy should be there soon."

Kevin nodded, and Adam changed the subject as they began moving.

"You're done working for the day?"

"Yeah," said Kevin, "I fed the cattle and we weeded the garden this morning. Dad said I could have the rest of the day off when we finished, so I got out of the yard fast before he changed his mind."

Adam chuckled, knowing that Mike Baranov could always find more work to be done.

In no time they had pulled into Adam's driveway, propped their bikes against the garage door and gone inside. A few minutes later the other two arrived.

After everyone was seated, Adam told the group about the events of the previous day.

"So you think Ben is the one that went through your house?" asked Kevin.

"Well, Elianora did say that Aeturnum always wanted more time to study the Heartstone. Ben must have heard the rumours that I might have it and that tattoo says he must be a member."

"Maybe he just wants to steal the Heartstone and sell it," said Jimmy. "I'm guessing that this Aeturnum group would pay pretty well."

The others looked at Jimmy full of suspicion.

"Come on, like you haven't thought that it would be nearly priceless. Besides, I know Adam doesn't have it anyway," he replied to their accusing looks.

"Yeah, but that's just daydreaming. This is the real thing. Someone actually broke into Adam's house," said Mark.

Adam and Kevin looked at each other, remembering the treasures hidden in Elianora's barn under all of the tarps. A lot of those items looked priceless too. That was one of the other details they left out when they re-told the story of the previous summer, although they would rather have had people find out about the treasure than their adventure on the flowery bicycle.

"The strange thing was how neatly he pulled everything out of the cupboards and went through them. It didn't take me more than an hour to clean it all up again. That by itself makes me suspect Ben. Everything he does is neat and orderly, so I would assume he would search a house the same way," said Adam.

Everyone agreed except for Kevin. "There are a few people around this town that are as big of neat freaks as Ben, though. I just can't see him doing that. My parents trust him completely," he said.

Adam nodded, "I know. I'm not 100 percent convinced that he is guilty, but you have to admit that he's pretty high on the list of suspects. If we didn't know that Larix was somewhere else, I wouldn't even think it was Ben. The fact that he came and got me to fix his lawn mower this morning was odd enough behaviour. It felt weird, and now that I'm talking about it, I have a theory as to why."

The others looked at Adam with curiosity.

"I think he was hoping that I would tell him about the break-in and confide in him where the Heartstone really is, being that he is the head of security," Adam finished.

It took a short time for the others to have the theory sink in.

"That's a pretty convincing point," said Jimmy.

"It could have just been coincidence," said Kevin, but not sounding like he was convinced himself.

"It could be," said Adam, "but it's a pretty crazy coincidence if that's all it is."

They sat in a group silence again, each processing the information. A minute later Mark was the first to speak.

"What now? After seeing what he did to those guards last year, I'm not really excited to march over to his house and start accusing him, especially if he *is* guilty. That'd be like poking a rabid skunk with a short stick – and if he isn't guilty it would just be like poking a regular skunk with a short stick."

The others grinned at his observation.

"We've got to tell someone," said Kevin. "Someone high enough up the chain of command to be able to do something."

"Are you thinking Elianora?" asked Adam.

Kevin nodded.

Mark interrupted. "Well, you'll have to wait. Dad and her are gone until tonight."

"Gone? I know your dad travels sometimes, but I didn't think Elianora ever left her house," said Adam.

"That's what I thought too. This must be something important if they both have to go," replied Mark.

"Who does that leave that we trust?" asked Adam.

The others looked at each other.

"Well, there's Don Chen – he *is* Number 3. He should probably be next on the list," said Kevin.

Jimmy shook his head. "The Chens are gone on vacation. They left last week and won't be back for a few more days."

Adam looked deep in thought. "Who else?" he asked.

"Both of your parents," said Mark, pointing at Kevin and Jimmy.

"But my parents won't listen because they trust Ben so much, especially after last summer," said Kevin.

"Mine too," echoed Jimmy.

The group was quiet again as they thought of options.

"I guess that leaves Marius and Karl," said Adam. "Last year Elianora said that Karl was the one who hid the Impression Stone in Grayson, so she must trust him a lot."

"Marius will be busy at work today, so we wouldn't be able to talk to him until later. Karl works from home," said Mark.

"Karl it is," said Adam.

The rest of the group agreed.

Adam had grown to like Karl over the past year through their shared love of Kurling. The times that Karl had taken Adam out to practice had really improved his game. Adam didn't usually lose too badly anymore.

After they had stepped outside, Mark started to get on his bike.

"We don't have to ride our bikes. We can just walk," said Adam.

Mark groaned.

"He's not even a block away if we take the alley," said Adam as the other two shook their heads.

"Oh yeah, I forgot," said Mark, trying to cover his whining.

"I swear you must still wear diapers because you're too lazy to walk to the bathroom," said Kevin.

"Ha ha," is all that Mark replied, knowing that if he said any more the teasing would continue.

"Well, now that Mark's heart rate is up we should probably go," added Jimmy with a smirk.

Mark rolled his eyes while Adam suppressed a chuckle. A few seconds later they were making their way south down the alley. Karl's house was on the opposite side of the alley and on the opposite end of the block.

As the group walked past Karl's back fence, Karl stepped out his side door.

"Karl," Adam yelled to get his attention.

Karl looked around, startled by the yell. In a moment he had located the source and he began to smile as he looked quickly to each of the group.

"Boys, hello! What are you doing here?" he asked in his slight German accent as he wandered toward them.

"We were wondering if you had a minute for us to talk to you about something," replied Adam.

"Sure. Come in." He pointed at the back gate.

Karl met them in his back yard, seeming happy to have visitors.

"So what can I help you with?" He asked once they were all inside. "You want some extra Kurling lessons?" His great chin wiggled as he spoke.

Adam shook his head. "No. We need to talk to someone senior in the League about a concern, so we thought we would see if you were home first before we talk to anyone else."

Karl seemed surprised and happy at hearing that, but the look on his face changed, as if he remembered something. He looked at his watch and shrugged. "I guess I can take a couple of minutes to talk. Let's just step inside the garage for a little bit of privacy." Karl unlocked the side door and stepped in, turning on the lights as he motioned them all to follow.

The garage was larger than it had looked from the outside, probably because Karl's car was so small. Everyone used to tease Karl about the small vehicles he preferred to drive, but he would promptly remind them that the cars in Europe were about the same size. Because Karl was so overweight, though, it looked like a clown car to most of the children in town.

"What are your concerns," Karl asked as he closed the door.

Adam looked to his friends who seemed to have already expected that Adam was going to do the talking. Adam began telling the story about the break-in the previous night and ended with fixing Ben's lawn mower.

"So you didn't tell your mom about the break-in?" asked Karl.

Adam shook his head and said, "No."

Karl stood still, deep in thought. "And you think Ben did it," he said, more as a statement than a question. "So, what do you think he was looking for? You've said that you never found the real Heartstone, only the fake."

"Yeah, but I don't think everyone believes me. We think he was either looking for the Heartstone or my dad's lapel pin for some reason."

Karl considered the information for a moment. "I'm glad you came to me first boys. You probably should have told your mom, Adam, but in this circumstance, maybe it will be better that you didn't. Not too many people in this town would believe you if you said anything bad about Ben, especially your parents." He looked at each boy in turn before continuing.

"I would agree that it was probably Ben that searched your house. I've never completely trusted him. You saw his tattoo, so you know that he was a member of Aeturnum. What you don't know is that he was their head of their security before coming here. Even I don't know much else about his history, but I do know that he has been to jail in the past for breaking and entering."

Adam got a chill as he remembered the comment from Ben about going to court before.

Karl looked at Adam. "Tell me *exactly* what the message said inside the fake Heartstone. Don't hold anything back or try to hide anything. I need to know in order to decide what we should do next."

Adam told him the message exactly and described the picture at the end. Karl had closed his eyes and listened intently, looking up only after Adam was finished describing the symbol.

"Ok, so what did you see in the Impression Stone you found in Killaly?"

Adam shrugged. "Nothing. I didn't get a chance to connect with it, and I didn't even think about trying, to be honest. I thought it would just be the same instructions as the other one."

Karl nodded again, closing his eyes once more in thought. After a few moments he began to nod.

"Well, I am pretty sure I know what we should do next, but I need to know you boys are willing to trust me. You could get in pretty big trouble with your parents if you get caught. Do you want to hear more?"

The boys looked at each other. They remembered the excitement from the previous year as they hunted for clues, finding the tunnels and risking being caught. It had been exciting and scary at the same time. Each boy nodded to their group before nodding at Karl.

"Great," said Karl.

"So, here's what I think we need to do. That second Impression Stone is important. You didn't know it, but Elianora was very adamant that we retrieve it. She sent most of us senior members to try and get it. Most of us tried multiple times. We even had to let John Gunderson in on the fact that something important was 'protected' by the good people of Killaly. I think Elianora knows it has information on it that will help her find the actual Heartstone again, so what we need to do is clear. I think Adam needs to connect with the other Impression Stone to see if there is any difference between the two."

Adam winced. It would have been much easier to connect with it when it was sitting in his pocket the previous day instead of now when it was somewhere in Elianora's house. The thought hadn't even entered his mind with everything else that had gone on in Killaly.

"That's not going to be easy," said Adam. "I gave it to Elianora last night and she put it in a box with the other Impression Stone."

Karl gave a nod as he absorbed the facts.

"I know she's gone today and it was a last minute trip, so I'll bet it has to do with what she found in the Impression Stone, although who she's seeing or where she had to go is a mystery to me," said Karl, "and I'll bet she either took them with her or hid them somewhere that we won't be able to find them. Knowing her, she won't let them get too far from her yet."

"Dad went with her, and they are supposed to be back by supper time," added Mark.

Karl nodded silently, thoughts obviously running through his head. After some time, he spoke again.

"And Ben knows that too or he'd have been there as soon as she left this morning instead of getting you to fix his mower. I wonder - if *you* asked her," he pointed at Adam, "she might let you see them again." Karl seemed to be working things out as he spoke.

"Maybe you'd get enough time to connect with it if your friends could provide a distraction," he continued.

"You think that she would let me see them if I just asked?" asked Adam.

"If there's one thing I know about her, she trusts everyone more than she should, and I know she has a soft spot for you – especially after last summer. My biggest worry is that she will just hand them over to Ben if he asked because she trusts him so much," said Karl.

It sounded reasonable to Adam, but he had another thought.

"I think we can do it, but the first Impression Stone only showed me images as I made my way through the Radome caves. Won't the Killaly Impression Stone be the same?" asked Adam.

"You might be right, but *you* can connect with the stones much better now than you could last year. I haven't seen that deep of a connection since your father. You might have a strong enough connection now that you can see the difference."

"Hang on just a second," interrupted Jimmy. "Aren't we here because we suspect Ben broke into your house?" he asked Adam. "Now we're planning on fooling Elianora to see the Impression Stones again and possibly go into the Radome caves? I'm not seeing the reason here."

The boys looked at each other and realized that they were getting caught in the excitement of the moment.

Adam nodded. "Good point. Plus, why would Ben need to get the Impression Stone anyway? Didn't Aeturnum take the Heartstone? And he knew I didn't have the fake Heartstone, so what was he looking for?"

Karl grimaced. "There are a few things you don't know. Once you found the fake Heartstone message, Elianora sent Ben back to his old friends to see if he could track the real one down. According to Ben, they don't have it, and if they did take it, they wouldn't have left such an obvious clue. They would have taken it and ran. You see, after the mid 1950's, Aeturnum wasn't given any more chances to study the Heartstone. They were told that the reason they couldn't was the manpower required to make sure it was safe. They've been asking and asking, but every time it was being studied it was in danger of being found by Larix again – too many people knowing where it is makes for loose security. Elianora is torn because while she wants to help Mankind evolve as much as possible, she also feels she needs to protect us. She believes more and more that the next time Larix gets the Heartstone, he's planning on killing the rest of the Teneo and half the population of the earth. So she has decided to keep it hidden since then. Aeturnum meanwhile has grown into a large company, known for a lot of food product innovation and chemicals. They've advanced quite a lot in the last number of years and believe that they should get another crack at the Heartstone – but Elianora has outright refused to ever let them see it again. Kevin would know them well – they *are* the biggest agricultural chemical manufacturer in the world."

Kevin thought for a moment. "Aeturnum is Mon-gill?"

Karl nodded. "And their start came as the result of studies related to the Heartstone. While they couldn't figure out how to make it work as a weapon, they did discover that it helped evolve the plants that were exposed to it. They developed new versions of agricultural plants that were much heartier and higher yielding, all as a direct result of having the Heartstone on site. Those seeds made them a lot of money, and now they have the resources to pay handsomely for getting the Heartstone back again."

Karl paused and took a deep breath before continuing.

"I think you were right that Ben was looking for your dad's pin. We were all beginning to think that your dad's pin was the key to unlocking Brutus, even though we have all tried our own pins. All of the Sentinel League lapel pins aren't created exactly equal. I mean, most of them are the same, but a few are slightly different. Your dad's is one of those that is different. It's much stronger than the others and has slightly different properties, so that's why we thought it might work."

The news about his lapel pin came as a shock to Adam. He wondered why Elianora and Gurpreet let him keep it if they knew how special it was.

"You still have it, right?" asked Karl.

"I keep it well hidden," Adam replied. He didn't tell Karl that most of the time he kept the pin in his pocket or under his pillow at night.

"I'm assuming that you needed your dad's lapel pin to open the statue?"

Adam shook his head. "Nope. I had to connect with the statue to get instructions on how to open the mouth."

"Really?" questioned Karl. "Interesting."

"So you think the symbol in the fake Heartstone was a diversion?" asked Adam.

"Yes. At least, that's what the senior members think now. I've discussed this with them too, and we think there are clues hidden in the Killaly Impression Stone and that's why Elianora wanted it back so much. My feeling is that the fake Heartstone was actually an intentional diversion by Elianora. I also think she wiped her memory of it afterwards."

Adam thought Karl was on to something, but still had concerns. "Won't Elianora just figure out the clues and have a team retrieve the Heartstone? I saw her read the Impression Stone with ease, so she must have figured it out already."

"Well, you know her. If she is the only one who knows the clues leading to it, she won't be in a panic to find it anytime soon. You know her theory about the fewer people that know about a thing the less likely it will be leaked. She'll take her time and plan out her next move. The problem is that Ben will want to know right away. He will ask her if he can protect the Impression Stones, being the head of security, and she'll give them to him. He'll have the Impression Stones figured out and tip off Aeturnum without her being any the wiser. As soon as Aeturnum finds the Heartstone, they'll pay Ben and he'll be gone. That's my theory anyway."

"I thought there were very few people who could read an Impression Stone," said Adam.

"Contrary to what you've been led to believe, the ability to read an Impression Stone isn't as rare as you think. And with the resources Aeturnum has, they'll find someone that can read them if Ben doesn't know someone already."

"But isn't Aeturnum just members of the Sentinel League? It shouldn't be a big problem if they find the Heartstone," said Jimmy.

"Well, if they happen to find the Heartstone first, how long do you think it will take for Larix to find out? He found out about Grayson when barely anyone knew it was here. Since Ben has left, Aeturnum's security is far from great. If a couple hundred researchers start talking because they aren't necessarily all Sentinel League members anymore, he'll have it in no time. "

That information hit Adam. He now understood Karl's logic.

"So that's why we need to get the information off that other Impression Stone as soon as we can. Elianora's insistence on finding it tipped off Ben to its importance which in turn tipped off Aeturnum, so we need to do something quick. If we can locate the Heartstone maybe we can set a trap to prove to Elianora that we are right. She already has arrangements for the next location it will be moved to, so we just have to find it and secure it before anyone else does. Does that answer your questions?"

The boys slowly agreed.

"Good. I think that you need to read the Killaly Impression Stone tonight, as soon as Elianora gets back." said Karl.

Adam nodded as his stomach tightened. Everything was starting to move fast again, as it had the previous summer, but this time he wasn't sure he'd be as lucky.

"How are we going to distract Elianora?" asked Mark. "She's got eyes in the back of her head."

The boys agreed.

Karl frowned. "The stories I heard about your adventures last summer said that you guys are pretty good at causing a distraction if you need, or are those stories wrong?" He paused as they thought about it. "I have no fear that you can come up with something before you get there."

The boys nodded slowly once more.

Karl looked at his watch again. "Anyway boys," he said as he pressed the button to open the garage door, "I've got a meeting to get to. Insurance sales is a 24 hour, 7 day-a-week business. I'll be back after lunch tomorrow. Do what you can this evening and come see me tomorrow afternoon, ok?"

They nodded and Karl smiled back at them.

"Good luck," he said as he ushered them out the big garage door.

CHAPTER TWELVE

The boys walked to the end of the driveway and stepped off to the side as Karl backed his little car onto the street. Karl honked his horn happily at them as he drove away.

"Back to your place?" Kevin asked Adam as they waved at Karl.

"Yep."

A couple of minutes later they were all seated in their usual spots.

"Well now, just how does he expect us to distract her long enough for you to connect with that stone?" complained Mark.

Jimmy agreed.

"It shouldn't take long for me to connect with it," replied Adam, "but it might take time to connect with it deep enough that I can tell the difference between the two. I might only need ten seconds, but as much as a couple of minutes."

They all sat quietly, listening to the birds chirping outside and the gentle breeze rustling the trees.

143

"Is there anything we want to ask her?" asked Kevin, breaking the silence. "You know, like, I'm curious how those books work. Those pages are paper thin and yet I could watch video on them."

"I'd like to know that too," agreed Mark.

"Well I've been curious about that tree that grows all different types of fruit at the same time. That's nothing I've ever even thought possible before," said Jimmy.

They all nodded again.

"Do you think that asking her for those answers would distract her long enough to give me some time?" asked Adam.

"Maybe," replied Kevin. "I think we'll have to try it and see. You think you could get her to take you outside to see that tree, Jimmy?"

Jimmy grinned his used car salesman grin. "Not a problem. How about we get Mark to warm her up with a question about the video pages, then you say that you and Kevin want to see the Impression Stone because Kevin saw the other one last year and is curious, then me and Mark will get her outside to see that tree. As soon as we get outside, Kevin can be your lookout. That should get you enough time, right?"

Adam nodded. "You know Jimmy, sometimes your schemes scare me in a bad way." Jimmy's smile faded a little. "But this time it scares me in a good way. I say we give it a try."

Jimmy's smile shone even more than before.

"Ok, so we know that Gurpreet is with Elianora at the moment and they are supposed to be home by supper time. Mark, can you go home and as soon as your Dad gets back and you've eaten, come and get us."

Mark nodded.

"You two," he pointed at Jimmy and Kevin, "maybe eat something early and meet me back here. I'll just wait in the garage for you until then. It's just after 2:00pm now, so try and get back here by 5 if you can. Tell your parents we're just hanging out."

The other two nodded in reply.

"I don't think I need to get home before 4:00," said Mark.

Adam thought about it for a second. "Yeah, I guess you're right. It would look suspicious if we all hung out at home on a nice day like this, especially since Kevin just left his house. What should we do to kill some time?"

"We could go to the store," said Mark. "I don't know about you guys, but I'm starting to get hungry."

Adam waited for Kevin or Jimmy to shoot Mark down, guessing it would be good.

"How can you be hungry already? You just ate lunch like an hour ago," said Kevin.

"It's all this excitement. It makes me feel like snacking on something," said Mark. He smiled and looked at Kevin. "And besides, that was just my first lunch."

Kevin looked at Mark with wide eyes. "Did you just make another 'Lord of the Rings' reference?" He hung his head.

Adam chuckled as Mark grinned back at Kevin.

"Why don't we just wander around to kill some time," said Jimmy.

They all looked at each other and each shrugged.

"Why not," said Adam, and he pointed the way outside.

The boys began walking toward downtown, if you wanted to call it that. Downtown consisted of the post office, hardware store, the hotel, the bank, and the butcher shop. It was almost two blocks long if you included the gas station.

As they walked, a few cars drove past. Each one of the drivers waved to the group as is typical in a small town. Everyone knew everyone almost too well.

They stopped outside the post office to check out the bulletin board. A couple of items for sale, a few old business cards from salesmen that drove through every now and then. Nothing new had been added in a couple of weeks, so they continued on toward the grocery store.

"Hey," a familiar voice yelled at the group.

Adam turned toward the sound. It came from the butcher shop. Marius Miller was standing in the doorway waving for the group to come toward him. Marius was the owner of Miller's Meats, famous for their hand-made sausage simply known as 'Miller's Sausage'.

The boys looked at each other quickly and waited for Adam to lead the way across the street, unsure what Marius wanted. Marius smiled and stepped fully outside as they approached.

"Hi guys," he said. "You looked like you're bored. How would you like to make some money?"

Adam wasted no time responding. "Sure!" he said.

Kevin nodded, Jimmy shrugged and Mark eyed Marius with suspicion.

"What's the job?" asked Mark.

Marius chuckled. "Nothing too bad. I just had a load of firewood delivered to my house and I need it stacked inside my shed. With the four of you, it shouldn't take more than an hour. I'll pay you each..." he told them a number.

Adam was more than happy with the amount for an hour of work, but Jimmy had other ideas.

"Well, that's alright, but I think it's worth a bit more...," Jimmy started.

Marius cut him off. "That's more than minimum wage and that's all I'll pay."

Jimmy closed his mouth and nodded.

"So you'll do it?" asked Marius.

All four boys agreed, even Mark.

"Good. Then follow me."

Marius led them back in the direction they came, since his house was in that direction only a block away from his business. As they approached, they could see a pile of wood that had been dumped on his driveway.

"If my kids were a little older I would get them to do it, but they're at their Grandma's house this week and I need this cleaned up before my wife gets home," said Marius as they walked up the driveway. Marius stepped around the pile, past a wheelbarrow and into the back yard where he stopped at an old tin shed before he turned to the boys.

"The easiest way to do this is for one of you to load the wheelbarrow, one of you run the wheelbarrow back and forth and make a pile at the door, and the other two stay in the shed and stack. It should go pretty quick that way."

"I'll run the wheelbarrow," said Kevin.

"I'll load you up," said Adam before anyone else could offer.

"That puts you two in the shed," said Marius. Mark had a small scowl on his face, but he would have scowled at any job he was given anyway.

"If you two can start getting some wood here, I'll show these guys how to stack it," said Marius.

Adam and Kevin made their way back to the wood pile.

After Kevin had taken a few of loads to the shed, Marius came back to the pile.

"When you're done, just come see me at the shop," he said, then turned and walked away.

"Poor Jimmy," chuckled Kevin, "he'll be doing most of it himself I'll bet."

Adam smiled and continued loading the wheelbarrow. After half an hour, the pile was gone from the driveway, so Adam walked to the back yard to check on the progress. To his surprise, Mark and Jimmy had almost kept up with them. There was only a wheelbarrow full of wood left to stack, and soon Adam saw why. Each time Kevin had dropped off a load of wood, he jumped in the shed and helped stack before getting the next load. Adam shook his head and smiled.

A few minutes later they were on their way to the butcher shop to pick up their pay. The entire job had only taken them 45 minutes. When they stepped inside, Marius looked surprised that they were there.

"It's done?" he asked.

"Yep," said Jimmy.

"Wow. I should have done this sooner," he said, grinning. He reached into his pocket and took out some money, distributing it evenly to the boys.

"I'm going straight to the store. See you guys later," said Mark. He turned and nearly ran out the door.

"I'm going to follow him so I can mock his choices," said Jimmy, following soon after.

Adam turned to Marius. "Since I'm here, can I buy some sausage? Mom rarely brings any home and I love it."

Marius smiled, then opened the freezer door behind him and pulled out two packages, handing one to Adam and one to Kevin. Adam held out his hand to pay, and Marius put up his hand to stop him.

"I can't take this for free," said Adam. Kevin nodded in agreement.

"You two had the hardest jobs. Consider this a bonus because you stepped up and offered to do the hardest part."

Adam felt strange about the gift, but since Kevin was getting the same it didn't feel like it was just charity.

"It's good and fresh, so you can just take it home, boil it for 10 minutes and it's ready to eat," he continued.

The boys thanked Marius and left the building.

"Here," said Kevin as he handed his package over to Adam.

Adam gave him a questioning look.

"We have tons of this in our freezer, and this little package isn't enough for all of us," Kevin replied to the look.

Adam wasn't sure if Kevin was just saying that or not, but decided that he should accept the gesture and not insult him by turning it down.

"Thanks," said Adam as he took the package and continued walking.

After a couple more blocks they once again parted company. Soon, Adam stepped in the side door of his house.

"Mom," he called out. No answer. He forgot that she had only gone to work for the afternoon since Mr. Garagan had given her the morning off.

Being alone in the house, Adam got to work. He found three half-decent potatoes in the bag under the sink, peeled them and put them in a pot of water once it had boiled. He started another pot of water for the sausage, but didn't put it in quite yet as the potatoes were going to take some time. Next, he found a can of creamed corn and poured it into a small saucepan, covered it and put it on a third burner to slowly heat up.

He unwrapped the sausage and took a sniff. The smoky smell made his stomach rumble as he dropped it into the rolling water before checking the time on his watch. As he opened the fridge for the final ingredients, he remembered there was no milk left, so he would have to mash the potatoes using water instead.

As soon as the ten minutes was up, he drained the sausage and cut it into smaller pieces, putting half of them on his plate and leaving the rest in the pot with a cover on top. Next, he drained most of the water from the potatoes, added butter, salt and pepper, then mashed them, dished up half onto his plate and poured his portion of the creamed corn on top.

He turned off all of the burners and sat at the table to enjoy his meal. As he finished gobbling down the last bite, he heard a knock at the door.

"Just a minute," he said with a half-full mouth as he took his plate to the sink and finished chewing.

He opened the door to see Jimmy standing there, then looked at his watch and noticed it was almost 5:00.

"I checked the garage first, but you weren't there," said Jimmy.

"I just finished eating when you knocked," said Adam. "Let's go wait for the others."

They wandered to the garage as Jimmy recounted how he had followed Mark to the store and kept offering healthy alternatives to whatever Mark was looking at.

"I thought he was going to punch me already, but we saw his dad's car drive by so I ran home to get a bite to eat. I saw your mom there otherwise I wouldn't have checked the house."

"So that means Elianora should be home now. As soon as the other two get here, we'll head out," said Adam.

"Are we using the tunnels to get there?" asked Jimmy.

"I thought we would. It's much shorter that way."

"You still have your key to Town Hall?"

Adam nodded. "Don't you?"

"Nope. Mom confiscated it as soon as she found out about it. No big deal, because I know someone that's allowed to go into Town Hall whenever he wants."

Adam blushed a little.

"Don't feel bad. I prefer it like this. If we get into trouble while we're down there, I'll just blame it all on you," said Jimmy.

Adam smiled. *Typical Jimmy*, he thought.

A few minutes later Kevin arrived, followed shortly behind by Mark.

"Dad mentioned that Elianora is at home again," said Mark, "Didn't say much else, though."

"Alright then," said Adam as he looked at his watch. "It's 5:34 pm. Is it too early to go yet?"

"I think we want to make sure it's still light enough out that she can still show us the tree," said Jimmy.

Adam agreed. "Ok then, let's get going," he said, then stopped suddenly. The others stopped as well. Adam turned and walked back to his hiding spot, retrieved something and headed for the door.

"Can't forget the key or we won't be going anywhere," said Adam.

He stepped out of the garage as he slipped the key in his pocket, and the others followed him. As he walked down the driveway, the motion of someone walking to his right caught his attention. It was Mary. She shouldn't be home for another hour, he thought, but the sight of her made him stop in his tracks, and Mark ran into him.

"Hey," Mark complained, then followed Adam's gaze to see Mary approaching.

"You guys head toward Town Hall. I'll meet you there," said Adam.

"Ok," said Kevin as he glanced past Adam and waved to Mary. "See you in a few minutes."

Adam started to walk toward Mary as the others went the opposite way. Soon he had intercepted her and they both stopped.

"Hi," said Adam. "You're home early."

"It was really slow at the store today and one truck didn't show up, so we closed early," she replied. "You on your way out with the guys?"

Adam nodded.

"Did you eat?"

"Yeah. There are leftovers for you. We stacked some firewood for Mr. Miller and he gave us some free sausage."

"All you got was sausage for your work?" asked Mary.

"No, he paid us too." Adam answered.

"Ok. You had better catch up with your friends now."

Adam barely nodded before turning around and jogging in the direction the rest of his group had gone. As he rounded the corner past the skating rink, he could see the other three standing at the door to Town Hall. A moment later a familiar car raced past him, stopping right where the other boys were standing.

CHAPTER THIRTEEN

Mayor Jeff Wyndum stepped out of his car, grinning from ear to ear as he looked at the boys standing at the door. Normally he would have parked behind the building, but parking at the front made sure that his audience wouldn't have a chance to run away before he could get to them.

Adam seriously debated turning around and heading back home, but decided that it would be too cruel to let his friends have to listen to Jeff all alone. He jogged the rest of the way.

Jeff smiled at Adam as he approached. "Hi Adam. I was just telling your friends here that I have another couple of hours to work yet tonight. Special assignment from Elianora herself. What are you guys doing here? Come to ask me for more advice?"

Adam controlled his panting before he replied. "We're actually on our way out to see Elianora. Just figured we'd go say hello."

Jeff eyed him for a moment. "And you're going to take the tunnels because they're faster – especially since you don't have a license and can't drive."

"Right," said Adam. He hadn't thought about it that way, since he had never driven a car yet.

"What are we waiting out here for," said Jeff, and he stepped up to the door.

A minute later they were inside and walking down the long hallway.

"So you're going to see Elianora," muttered Jeff. "You know, I think I might tag along. I have a couple of questions for her."

Adam's heart sank. Jeff would probably get in the way of their plan, and Elianora might not bring out the Impression Stones with him around.

"We take the tunnel that goes directly to her. You know, the one where you have to crawl through that small crawlspace," said Adam, hoping Jeff was reluctant to get on his hands and knees to crawl through, just like Gurpreet and Don had been.

Jeff thought about it for a moment. "Yeah. Actually, I should probably just get some work done. I can talk to her next week."

Adam tried not to show his excitement, and the rest of the boys said nothing.

"Besides, I can't really talk to her with *you* guys there. Pretty important stuff. I can't say anything about it though – it's just between me and her."

"Ok. We won't ask so we don't get you in trouble," replied Jimmy.

When they had reached the back of the building, Jeff turned to his office and the boys turned the opposite direction.

"I'm pretty sure you don't need me to take you into the basement," said Jeff, "so we'll see you when you get back.

I'll still be here working, so pop in and I'll take a break." He smiled at them and winked.

Adam nodded before turning toward the basement stairs, thinking about another route home to avoid Jeff on the return, although this time he hadn't been nearly as annoying as usual.

After turning on the lights, Adam led the way down the long, steep staircase into the cavernous basement. The familiar smell of old wood and damp paper flooded his nose as he took the last step.

"I think this place is even *creepier* now that I know it has that secret entrance to the tunnels," said Mark with a shiver.

The other boys agreed since they all felt the same.

They wove through the decorations in the storage room after fighting with the old storage room door, and soon they stood in front of the wood panel where their adventure had begun the previous year. Adam placed the pin in the impression, and the drawbridge door slowly fell open.

"I still think that's cool," said Adam as he watched.

"I bet he's stood here and just watched it open and close before," said Jimmy, looking to Kevin and Mark.

Adam blushed. He had actually done that very thing when he returned from seeing Elianora about his dream a few months prior, but he wasn't about to admit it anytime soon.

Instead, he said, "Let's keep moving."

Once he had stepped through the doorway, he gently stroked the wall in an upward motion and the ceiling began to glow. Next, he made his way over to the sliding door and placed the pin, pulled the handle and slid it open before stroking the wall on the other side and lighting up the tunnels.

In a matter of minutes they were standing at the opening to the crawlspace.

"Ladies first," Jimmy said to Mark, who quickly leaned backwards so that it looked like Jimmy pointed at Kevin.

"So you're offering to go first then?" asked Kevin as he raised an eyebrow. Mark laughed, and even Adam chuckled.

"I'll go first," said Adam. "It's really not a big deal."

"See, I told you it was ladies first," said Jimmy, getting a laugh out of Kevin and Mark.

In no time the group was through to the other side, but not before hearing Mark grunt his displeasure at using the crawlspace.

"We could have gone through the school, you know. It's not that much further," he complained as they continued walking. The rest of the group ignored him.

"So, everyone remembers the plan?" asked Jimmy after they had walked halfway to their destination.

"Yes, Mom," replied Mark, making the other two laugh.

"I'm being serious," said Jimmy. "I don't want to get there and all you do is ask her what she has in her fridge."

"That might not be a bad distraction," said Mark. "Now you've got me thinking just what *does* she have in her fridge? You can tell a lot about a person by what they keep in there, you know."

"I'll bet Ben has sauerkraut and severed fingers," said Jimmy.

The group chuckled.

"But seriously," continued Jimmy, "Mark what's first?"

Mark made every word sound like it pained him. "I ask her how the video's work in the books she showed us last year. Then these two yahoos get her to show them the Impression Stones, and the biggest yahoo of all gets her to take us outside to see her crazy fruit tree while we leave the others inside. Farmboy will serve as a lookout for when we return. Sound right?"

"Close enough," replied Jimmy, and they continued on their way.

It seemed like only a few minutes later that they arrived at the exit leading into Elianora's barn. It took Adam moments to open the inner and outer doors, and as soon as they stepped out, they heard Elianora call from the house.

"Hello! Come in the house boys."

Her voice startled each of them since they had expected to make it to the house and knock before hearing her. The shock didn't last long, and soon they were following Adam inside.

Elianora popped her head out of the kitchen once the last of them had stepped into the porch.

"Just grab a seat anywhere, ok? I'm making some lemonade."

After taking off his shoes and making it into the living room, Adam looked for a seat. He left the rocking chair open since it seemed to be the place Elianora always sat, so he sat in the chair nearest to it. Kevin and Mark sat on the sofa, and Jimmy sat on a small wooden stool. A moment later, Elianora arrived with a tray of drinks.

"I had just made myself a pitcher, so you came at the perfect time," she said as she handed each boy a glass.

Kevin elbowed Mark, since it seemed he forgot his manners.

"Uh, thanks," said Mark.

"You're welcome," replied Elianora. "So what brings you all the way out here?" she asked when she looked at Adam.

Adam thought quickly. "We were bored and thought we would come out for a visit...Actually, that's not totally true," he paused for a second. "We were sitting around and talking about all of the different things we've seen here, so we thought we'd come ask you a few questions, if you don't mind."

Elianora smiled. "Go ahead and ask. I don't mind at all."

Kevin was ready to elbow Mark again, but he remembered his part.

"I wanted to know how you get the video into those books. Those are paper thin pages, and each one showed a full video. Is it some kind of electronics that we don't know about?"

Elianora looked around. "That's a good question. Too bad I don't have one in the room at the moment. It's easier and harder than you think. Each of the pages in the book contains actual writing. We figured out a way of writing that goes straight to your brain and produces images. It's not your eyes that see the video, but that's how your brain processes it. Surprisingly enough, everyone processes the writing the same way. It is a very precise art and takes years to learn. It's easy to understand how it's done, but incredibly difficult to actually do properly."

Her answer was so quick that Mark didn't have a chance to get her to show him the books again, so he just nodded and said, "Cool."

After an awkward silence, Adam spoke next.

"I'm not sure if you'll let us do what I'm going to ask next, but I thought I'd ask," he paused as he looked at her. He felt as if she could read his mind and already knew his intentions. "Kevin and I were wondering if we could see the Impression Stone that I brought yesterday. In all of the excitement, I didn't really get to look at it, and because Kevin saw the other one last year, he's curious to see this one."

Elianora didn't move for a second, but then she smiled. "No problem," she answered, "I trust you guys."

The comment made Adam's gut clench as Elianora walked into the kitchen, returning with the box Adam had seen before. She opened it up and handed the box to him.

"They are both in there, along with the fake Heartstone. I had them with me today. Do you remember which one is which?" she asked.

Adam looked in and could tell which was which immediately by the sharp edge on the one from Killaly.

"This is the one I brought you yesterday," he said as he pointed in the box.

Elianora nodded. "You can take them out."

"Thanks," replied Adam as he took the one from Killaly and handed it to Kevin before taking the other one out for himself.

Jimmy jumped in, just as they had planned. "I wanted to ask if you could show me your tree in the yard that grows all the different fruits."

"And nuts," said Elianora.

"Really," said Jimmy, full of surprise. "Can you show me? I'm really curious how you were able to make it do that."

"Sure, let's go," she said and turned to the door.

Mark jumped up to follow. "I'm coming too. I don't want to sit here watching these two play with their stones."

Elianora grinned before turning back to Adam. "When you're done, just put them back in the box."

Adam nodded and returned to looking at the stone. As soon as he heard the screen door slam, he traded stones with Kevin. Kevin stood up and walked to the window where he could see through the curtains.

"Go for it," he said.

Adam cupped the stone in his hands, brought it up to his head and concentrated. He felt the familiar connection he got every time he had connected with the Kurling stones, but this connection was different. He could feel information loading into his brain, but when he tried to bring it to the front of his mind it felt like trying to grab smoke. He concentrated as hard as he could, slowly approaching the misty cloud of information, but every time he got close it moved away.

"They're coming back," he heard Kevin say.

He remembered the trick for seeing into mechanical things and tried to let his mind wander *into* the mist instead of trying to bring the mist to him. That didn't work either.

"They're at the door," said Kevin in a panic.

Adam popped out of his trance and resumed looking at the stone again as the others came back into the living room.

"Amazing," was all that Jimmy kept repeating.

Adam put the stone back into the box and then held it in front of Kevin while Kevin returned the other stone. He closed the box and handed it back to Elianora. He was disappointed that he had been unable to read the information on the Impression Stone and wondered how he would be able to try again, although he didn't think it would work. All that he could do now was go through the Radome caves and hope he could figure out the difference, even though he wouldn't have an Impression Stone to use in the last cave.

"Thanks," he said, and Elianora nodded as she took the box.

"Well, that's all we were wondering for now. I think we'll head back to Town Hall," said Adam, then he had another thought. "Jeff is waiting for us there. He's busy working on a project you gave him."

Elianora frowned. "Don't be too hard on Jeff. He's actually a really nice guy. He just has low self-esteem, so he tries to bring it up by bragging."

Adam didn't feel great. He knew deep down that Jeff was only trying to boost his own self-esteem, but it was really hard to deal with they way Jeff would brag so much.

"But in this instance, he actually isn't doing anything too important for the League, just helping me with my personal hobbies, and he has been really helpful. Just don't let him know that you know, ok?"

"So what is he doing?" asked Jimmy.

"He's trying to find some rare plants that I need for some experiments. He's really good at searching for things on the Internet. If I'm right, one could be as good of a discovery as when I invented the sealant you used on your shoes last year."

Adam remembered the stuff well. When it was applied to their shoes, they made no sound as they walked.

"You invented that?" asked Kevin.

Elianora nodded.

"Cool," said Kevin.

"So, like I said, just don't let Jeff know that you know, ok?"

Adam and the group agreed together.

"Ok. Thank you. Now, if you three will wait outside for a minute, I need to talk to Adam."

Jimmy, Mark and Kevin looked at each other like they didn't know what to do. Adam motioned for them to go, and they slowly moved to the door.

"We'll meet you at the barn," said Elianora as they walked outside.

Once they were gone, she picked up the box with the Impression Stones and handed the box to Adam.

Adam looked at her with surprise.

"I want you to look after these for me," she said.

"Why?" was all that Adam could ask.

"I trust you and I know you and Kevin are interested in them. I am going away for a couple of days and I want to make sure they are safe. Between you four boys I know nothing will happen to them."

"Really?" asked Adam. "Aren't you afraid we'll lose them or something?"

Elianora shook her head. "These are Impression Stones. Just connect with them. As long as you are the last one who has connected with an Impression Stone, you can call it back from wherever it might be, and you can connect with many of them at the same time. Right now I am connected to them, but as soon as you can you should connect with them all so you won't lose them."

"But what about the fake Heartstone?"

"What about it?" she asked.

"What if I lose it?"

"You won't lose it. It's actually made around an Impression Stone so you should connect with it too. It's just a fake, but I'd appreciate it if you don't lose it."

Adam agreed. He wanted to ask her why she wasn't giving them to Ben to look after, but thought that maybe she was beginning to suspect Ben after all and this was her way of hiding the stones.

"Good. Let's go meet your friends."

CHAPTER FOURTEEN

A few minutes later the group was headed back down the tunnel again. Kevin noticed the box that Adam was carrying right away, so he asked about it. Adam told the others what had happened as they walked.

"We went all the way out there and did all of that when you could have just come out here yourself and she would've handed them to you," said Mark complaining.

"How was I to know that she'd do that?" asked Adam.

"All that matters is that Adam has the Impression Stones and now he can figure out if there's a difference between them," said Kevin.

Adam thought back to his attempt in Elianora's living room. He was pretty sure that he was nowhere near skilled enough to find the difference, but soon he would be able to take his time and make sure.

As they arrived at the crawlspace, Adam led the way through again followed by Jimmy and then Kevin, with Mark on the end. As soon as they each exited, they started walking toward the junction until Mark howled in pain behind them.

They rushed back and saw Mark kneeling on the ground.

"What happened?" asked Kevin.

After a few grunts and a bit of rocking back and forth, Mark managed to say, "Hit my head."

Kevin rolled his eyes and sighed.

"You're supposed to get all the way out before you stand up," said Jimmy.

Mark waved a certain finger at him, making Jimmy smile.

"He'll be ok," said Jimmy.

They waited a little while longer and soon Mark got to his feet.

"You're not bleeding, at least. No blood means no problem, as my Grandma used to say." Jimmy chuckled at his own comment.

Mark smiled weakly and then motioned for the others to start walking.

When they turned to begin, a hulking figure entered the tunnel at the other end, startling them all.

"I should'a known it was you four makin all that noise. Thought someone was beating a cat with a hammer. Get out here," said Ben as he backed into the junction.

They boys did exactly as he said.

"Hello Sunshine," said Ben as Adam stepped past him.

Mark chuckled at the comment.

"What, are you jealous you don't have a nickname too? We can fix that pretty quick. I think Creampuff suits you."

Jimmy laughed at that, drawing Ben's attention.

"Feeling left out? Let me think. There's got to be something good for you too. Hmm... Aha! I'm gonna call you Lollipop because you're always looking for a sucker."

Jimmy's smile faded.

Ben looked to Kevin, but Kevin didn't say anything or even break a smile.

"This guy I like," was all Ben had to say about Kevin.

"So what are you doing down here and what's with all the noise?"

"We were bored so we went out to say hi to Elianora. Mark hit his head coming out of the crawlspace on our way back," said Adam.

Ben eyed him suspiciously. "Why would you want to go out there?"

"Why not?" answered Adam with a shrug. "Beats sitting around in my garage."

Ben seemed to accept this reasoning, but glanced at the box Adam was holding.

"What's in there?"

Adam panicked. He had forgotten about the box of stones and the lapel pin in his pocket – the very things Ben was looking for. He didn't have an answer.

Thankfully, Jimmy was quick.

"Elianora thought Adam could use an empty box to store parts in instead of her throwing it out," he said with a straight face.

Ben stared at Jimmy intensely, trying to read him. After a few seconds he seemed satisfied.

"You came in through Town Hall, I assume?" he said.

Adam nodded.

"Ok. Head on back there then," said Ben, pointing to the correct tunnel.

The boys wasted no time getting back to the file room. After fiddling around with the door a little to get it open, they stepped through and shut it tight behind them.

"Thanks Jimmy," said Adam.

"No problem. I'm just glad it worked," said Jimmy.

Mark nodded. "I don't know if my heart rate will slow down for another hour. That guy is scary."

"Let's just get out of here and go back to the garage," said Kevin as Adam opened the drawbridge door once more.

They raced up the stairs and toward the hallway before they remembered that Jeff was still there working. It was too late, though. Jeff had heard them coming and was opening his door as they got there.

"Back so soon," he said with a large grin that changed to a look of suspicion. "She didn't tell you what I'm working on, did she?"

Adam shook his head. "Nope. All she told us is that it is important and you're doing a great job so far."

Jeff beamed at the compliment. He almost didn't seem to know how to respond.

Almost.

"Well, that's why she asked me. She's been around here long enough that she's heard what I can do, and now she feels more comfortable asking – since we *are* on such good terms. I know she would have liked to invite me to join the League much earlier, but she realized that having me in the most powerful position in town was *way* more important. Especially since she knew I would always make the best decisions for the town and its people."

Adam nodded as Jeff talked. It was the nod of the trapped audience listening to a speaker who wouldn't pause or let anyone get a word in no matter how hard they tried. Jeff continued talking but Adam's mind was processing all the data he had recently learned.

"...so that's how I did it. Anyway, I should get back to work now. Can you lock the front door on your way out?" Jeff finished after a few minutes of rambling.

Adam almost missed it, but as soon as he realized he quickly replied, "Sure thing...Don't work too hard," and he began walking to the front door.

"I'd say that I never do, but you all know that would be a lie," replied Jeff. "Goodnight." He retreated back into his office and closed the door.

The boys hurried outside and walked fast for a few steps before returning to a normal pace. Adam looked at his watch and noticed that it was just after 8 pm.

"Again, that was painful," said Mark.

All the others agreed.

"Anyone have to be home early tonight?" asked Adam.

The rest of the group shook their heads.

"Dad's probably going to get me up early again," said Kevin, "so I don't want to be out too late."

"Ok. I just want to take a few more tries at the stone, and then we can decide what we want to do from there," replied Adam.

They hurried back to the garage, and as soon as they were seated Adam took out the Impression Stones. He gave one to Jimmy to look at, but kept the one from Killaly for himself. He stared at it for a moment wondering if there was some trick he needed to know in order to read it properly.

"Get on with it," said Mark.

"Alright alright," replied Adam, and he began.

Adam felt the familiar connection he had the first time he connected with the Impression Stone. This time, he didn't feel information loading into his brain, but he knew it was all still there because he could see the misty cloud in front of him. He concentrated as hard as he could, slowly approaching the misty cloud of information, but every time he got close it moved away.

Again, he tried to let his mind wander into the mist instead of trying to bring the mist to him, and again it didn't work. The tightness in his stomach told him he wasn't skilled enough to read the stone.

"It's no use. I can't do it," said Adam.

"Are you sure," asked Kevin.

Adam described to the others what it was like, and they were quiet for a while.

"So what can we do now?" asked Jimmy. "If you can't read it, how do we know if there's anything different on that stone?"

Adam sighed. "We go back into the Radome caves."

All were silent.

"Well," said Mark. "If that's the only way...Let me know how it went when you get back."

Kevin rolled his eyes.

"Oh, come on," exclaimed Jimmy. "There's no way you're missing out on this. You're coming with us."

"Why? Adam's the only one that's been in there before and he's the only one that can use the two stones," said Mark.

Jimmy considered it for a short while. "We need you to come just in case there's trouble. The more people we have, the safer we'll be."

Mark looked at Jimmy suspiciously, but his mouth slowly broke into a smile. "Yeah, I guess I'm kinda curious too. I'm in."

Jimmy grinned back at Mark. "And besides, you're kind of like the one of guys who wear red on Star Trek anyway."

They boys laughed as Mark faked being upset. They all knew the guys who wore red were the expendable characters on the show.

"Are we going in tonight?" asked Kevin.

Adam looked at his watch. "It's 8:30 now, and Jimmy needs to be home by 11..."

"11:30," Jimmy corrected.

"Ok, 11:30. It would be tight, but we could do it if we leave right now. The other option is to go in the morning. What do you think?"

"I have to work in the morning," said Kevin.

"I have to sleep in the morning," said Jimmy. Mark seconded his comment.

"I guess we go now," said Adam.

After shoving the stones in his pockets, he walked over to his toolbox, opened the top, and took out his large homemade flashlight.

"I thought there was light in the caves," said Mark. He looked confused.

"This isn't for the caves, it's for the ride home after," said Adam.

Mark's face lit with understanding while Jimmy and Kevin shook their heads.

"Let's go then," said Adam.

"You have everything?" asked Kevin.

Adam patted his pockets.

"The pin is in there too?" asked Kevin again.

Adam nodded.

"Weren't you worried when we met Ben?" asked Kevin.

"I forgot I had the box until he started giving nicknames to Creampuff and Lollipop here," said Adam.

Jimmy rolled his eyes.

Mark said, "Very funny, Sunshine."

"But seriously, yeah, I was pretty nervous."

"We got lucky," said Jimmy.

Adam nodded.

"Let's get moving," said Kevin.

They shuffled out the door, grabbed their bikes and were off.

"Which way is quicker – past the weather monitoring station or past Elianora's," asked Kevin.

"The monitoring station," said Mark. "We can take the back road straight to it, but it might be a little muddy. Dad used to drive that way to check on the Radome once in a while because he said that was where the sensors were located for the monitoring station. He always said that was the fastest way."

"See, I told you we needed you to come along. We didn't know that," said Jimmy.

Mark wasn't sure if he should smile or not, cautious about what teasing could be next.

"Lead on," said Adam, happy to hand over the lead to Mark.

Mark turned toward downtown, and the others followed close behind. Adam stayed at the back, glad that he was able to be last for once.

Just past the post office, two familiar shapes stepped out of the grocery store. Mark waved at the two old ladies first, and the other boys followed his lead.

Aggie scowled back at them, but Martha smiled and waved before noticing the scowl on Aggie's face. She nudged her short friend who gave a weak wave as a result.

Adam thought that it was strange for Aggie to be upset with them. After all, they *had* saved the townspeople not that long ago. He shrugged it off and kept pedaling, glad that they didn't wave him down with another ominous prophecy.

Mark kept a steady pace - not a fast pace - until they reached the monitoring station. When they did, he pulled into the driveway instead of turning down the back road.

"What's up," asked Jimmy.

"Just taking a break," replied Mark.

"Come on. You don't need a break. You've been riding slower than my grandma rides her electric scooter inside the grocery store the whole way," said Jimmy.

Mark looked at him and stuck out his tongue.

"Well, we're just going to keep on going, so we'll see you when you get there. I haven't seen the way that office building opens into the caves yet. I can't wait," Jimmy continued.

The other three boys turned toward the back road, and Mark hurried to catch up. His curiosity overrode his laziness.

Adam looked down the back road. It was a dirt trail with brush trees lining each side, barely wide enough for a vehicle to get through. The only difference between it and Elianora's driveway was that her driveway was lined with gravel.

It didn't take long for the boys to make it the rest of the way. Even though it had rained that morning, there were only a few mud puddles left that they skirted easily.

"Here's another place that was creepy before I knew about the caves and now it's extra creepy," said Mark from far behind the others. He puffed deep breaths as he strained to keep up.

Adam pulled into the driveway and parked beside the shed. The shed was on the opposite side of the Radome from the phony office building. Adam hadn't been back since the previous summer and nothing had changed except that there were more weeds growing at the edges of the property. The others copied his lead and soon they all stood at the side of the office.

Adam felt in his pocket and pulled out the pin before placing it in the hole at the base of the building. He fiddled around until it fit in the right spot, and he knew he had it when he heard the mechanisms moving again. When the sound stopped, he pulled up hard and the building pivoted upward.

"No way," said Mark, jaw hanging open at the sight. Jimmy looked the same.

"Told you guys it was cool," said Kevin.

"That's beyond cool," said Jimmy.

Adam nodded, grinning wide. Then he remembered something important.

"Ok. There's lots of cool stuff in here, but you have to make sure you stay behind me and do exactly what I say. I don't know how to get you out without telling Ben if you get trapped," Adam looked right at Mark as he spoke.

Mark seemed to understand the gravity of what might happen if he didn't listen so he nodded in agreement alongside the others.

"Alright then. If you don't remember, the stairs are in complete darkness and flashlights don't work. You can see up a little, but not down. Stay to the left and feel the wall as you go. There's a landing quite a way down before the second set of stairs, so when I get to it I'll tell you. We'll stop once everyone gets there before we continue, Ok?"

After seeing the nods from his friends, Adam began his descent into the darkness.

CHAPTER FIFTEEN

Memories took the place of sight in Adam's mind as he entered the complete darkness. He had been down this stretch of stairs twice before – once with Kevin and again with Larix once they had been caught returning up the stairs. Adam had made it all the way down to the landing that first time, but Kevin had only made it halfway down the 100 or so stairs before returning to the top. Larix and his men had arrived in that short time, and now that Adam thought about it, Larix's group most likely came down the same back road the group had used only half an hour ago. The brush trees would have provided enough cover for them until they were nearly there.

Adam remembered how terrible Kevin had felt afterward. Kevin tried not to tell Larix about the decoy stone in Adam's pocket, but the high dose of the drug he was given made some part of him blurt out everything he knew with no control. Adam had to convince Kevin that it worked out for the best in the end because their adventure in the Radome caves gave the others enough time to come to the rescue. Any less time and they would have all been dead.

Another part of that memory brought Adam back to reality. That first time they had tried, Kevin had been afraid of descending the stairs in the dark.

"How's everyone doing back there," said Adam mainly so he could check on Kevin.

"Fine," said Jimmy from further up.

"Ok," said Mark from somewhere even further than Jimmy.

"Just don't stop 'til you get to the landing, ok?" said Kevin from close behind.

"Ok," agreed Adam, happy that Kevin was making progress.

Adam cursed in his head since he had forgotten how many steps he had taken so far. "Anyone counting the steps?" he said.

"Nope," came three replies.

Adam thought he had to be close the bottom and guessed he was probably three-quarters of the way. As he settled in for twenty or thirty more steps, he stumbled as he hit the landing.

The instant both feet touched down, an image appeared in his mind. Like the last time, It was as though the lights had been turned on for a second giving him a view of the entire staircase ahead. Straight in front of him was the large hole. Unlike the last time, the hole was on the opposite side.

"I'm there," he called back up the stairs.

Moments later he heard Kevin's footsteps reach the landing. Jimmy and Mark weren't too far behind. All of them had come down on the left side.

"How's everybody doing?" asked Adam.

"This is freaky," said Mark.

"I'd use something stronger than freaky," said Jimmy.

"I think it was worse this time, and I already knew what to expect," said Kevin.

Adam was surprised at the three since he hadn't found it that terrible, especially since he thought he knew where the danger was. Maybe connecting with the Impression Stone helped him deal with it better than the others somehow.

"The next part is exactly the same, but the hole has switched sides from last year so we have to go to the right side wall."

"How could it switch sides? It's a hole?" asked Jimmy.

"I don't know, but that's what the vision showed me."

"And you're sure it was on the other side last year?" asked Kevin this time.

"Absolutely. If it hadn't been, I would have fallen into it when I ran back up the stairs last year."

"How do you get a hole to change sides?" asked Mark.

"I don't know, but I need to make sure I don't take anything for granted from now on, and you all need to stay behind me," replied Adam.

"Yes please," said Mark.

"The good thing is that by the time you get to the last couple of steps, I'll have the Lumiens started and we can see from there on." He tried to sound like it was no big deal as he was telling them, but he didn't think it worked too well.

"Ok, I'm on my way across," he said.

Adam cautiously felt for the edge of the landing before following it over to the other wall. Soon he felt the right hand wall and was relieved.

"Make your way across the landing to me, then keep your hand on the right hand wall as you step down."

He listened to feet shuffling across and kept his hand out to feel for anyone as they approached. Seconds later he grabbed a hand and guided it to the wall.

"Thanks," said Kevin.

"I'm at the wall," said Mark.

"Me too," said Jimmy.

"Ok, here I go. I'll yell if I fall," Adam joked. His humour brought no laughs in the dark.

The first few steps were the worst as Adam felt lightly for each step before he would put any weight down. He didn't completely believe the visions, although they hadn't steered him wrong before. It just made no sense how the hole in the stairs could shift sides over the past year. Step after step went the same way, and after 20 or 30, he regained a lot of his confidence, returning to his previous pace until he reached the landing. As he swiped his hand upward and the Lumiens glowed to life, he breathed a sigh of relief.

Moments later, Kevin jumped off the last step. The relief of being able to see again showed on his face. He stepped forward a couple of steps so he wouldn't be in the way of the other two and looked around. His face changed from relieved to amazed.

"You know I trust you and all, but unless you see it, it's hard to believe," he said.

"I know," said Adam.

Jimmy stepped off the bottom step with the same look on his face that Kevin had.

"Wow," was all he said as he looked around.

He stepped further into the cave, mesmerized by what he saw. Adam looked around too, and saw that it was actually quite impressive. The cave was the size of a football stadium and lit eerily by the Lumiens. The first time he had been there he hadn't been able to just observe what a huge structure someone had built. It was a cave, but it was obviously man-made.

Jimmy took another step away from the stairs and into the cave when Adam stopped him.

"There shouldn't be any traps up to the edge of the cavern, but I'd like to check it out first before you go," said Adam.

Jimmy paused when he realized that he had been mesmerized by just looking around. "Thanks," was all he replied.

The three waited and waited, but Mark didn't seem to be coming.

Just as Adam was going to call out to him Mark's shoe appeared on one of the steps, cautiously and carefully making sure there was a step in front before he would commit to the next one.

"Get down here," said Jimmy, "It's fine."

Mark didn't speed up at the comment, but it didn't matter because in two more steps he was at the bottom. Like the other two, relief washed over his face to be replaced next by wonder. He stared forward with his mouth hanging open, and slowly took a couple of steps forward. As he was about to pass Adam, Adam grabbed him.

"Whoa there," said Adam, "let me make sure it's safe first."

Mark snapped back to reality and nodded. He closed his gaping mouth and turned it into a smile.

"Go to it," he said to Adam, "I wanna check this place out. This is like the mines of Moria." Excitement rang in his voice.

Kevin looked at Mark. "Am I going to have to listen to a bunch of Lord of the Rings references just because we're in a cave?"

Mark grinned. "Absolutely."

"You need to get out more," said Kevin.

"Like you haven't seen the movie," said Mark.

Kevin shook his head. "Nope."

Mark's eyes widened. "What? You're kidding."

"I'm not kidding. I have not seen any one of the movies," said Kevin.

"Man, are you missing out," said Mark.

Kevin shrugged.

"Kev, make sure these two stay here while I check the area," said Adam.

Kevin just nodded, but he was staring around almost as much as the other two.

Adam shrugged before he began searching all around. He remembered that ahead of them was a cavern that seemed to be bottomless, and the only way over it was a bridge on the far left wall. The bridge had a trap door that would open if you didn't run over it fast enough. The memory of the hole in the stairwell shifting from one side to the other gave him a hunch that maybe the bridge shifted too. Because of that, just like the last time, he began his search on the right side of the stairs and worked his way along the wall until it turned, leading him to the far right hand wall. When he reached the spot near where the bridge should be, he had another vision. This time it was identical to the first time he had come into this cave. It showed him a bridge part-way across the cavern on the right hand side of the cave, and a bridge that extended across the entire cavern on the left.

Careful that he didn't get ahead of himself, he worked his way back along the wall exactly the way he came, feeling the entire surface to make sure he didn't miss anything. Once back at the stairway he made his way over to the left side and continued in the same way.

He made it all the way to the left wall by the bridge before triggering the exact same vision he had on the right wall.

"Ok, it's safe. Come over to me and stay against the wall."

Kevin, Mark and Jimmy made their way over.

"Now you're gonna tell me that there's an invisible bridge there?" said Mark as he pointed.

Adam nodded and took a step onto the bridge. To the others it looked like Adam was floating in mid-air. "See," he said.

"That is so freaky," exclaimed Mark.

"You guys wait there until I find the next trigger, then come up to me but stay in line and stay next to the wall. This bridge is only about 2 feet wide."

Adam crept up the bridge, feeling the wall the whole way. He didn't want to take a chance and miss something, so he kept using the same pattern of feeling the entire wall until he found the trigger. Again, nothing had changed from the previous year. The instructions showed that you needed to run over the trapdoor and if you weren't fast enough it would open before you made it across.

"Come on," said Adam, waving to his friends.

The three looked at each other.

"Well, if neither of you are going to," said Jimmy. He stretched his foot out and touched it down lightly. When he seemed satisfied that something actually *was* there, he took another slow step. Once he was fully on, he bounced up and down a little to make sure it held his weight and then continued carefully toward Adam.

"You're next Cupcake," said Kevin.

Mark rolled his eyes, but followed behind Jimmy. Kevin stepped on as soon as Mark had gone a little way.

"Once you're on a little way, turn around and look back," said Adam.

A few steps later the three stopped and turned around.

"Oh, wow," said Kevin, "I can see it."

"Yeah, the illusion only works in one direction," said Adam.

The three boys turned back toward Adam and continued walking. Suddenly, Mark stopped dead, turned around and faced Kevin. He brought his hands together above his head as if he was holding a long pole, then brought them down as if smashing the pole into the ground. Kevin stared at Mark as if Mark had gone insane, but Mark stared back at him and said, "Balrog of Mordor – YOU SHALL NOT PASS!"

Kevin looked at him, shock and disbelief on his face.

"You didn't...," was all Kevin could stammer out.

Mark laughed hard at Kevin's frustration.

"You guys won't mind if I push him off here, right?" said Kevin.

"Go ahead," said Jimmy, "because if you don't, I will."

Mark was still smiling as he turned back toward Jimmy and Adam and kept walking. "You guys have no sense of humour."

"The only problem with your little re-enactment was that it wasn't the fat hobbit that said that - it was Gandalf," said Kevin.

Jimmy and Adam laughed hard.

Mark stammered for a moment until he regained his thoughts. "You said you never saw the movie."

"I didn't."

"So, how would you know that?" asked Mark.

"There are these things called 'books' you know," said Kevin.

"You've read 'The Lord of The Rings'?" asked Mark.

"I've read lots of books," said Kevin.

"But you have terrible marks at school," said Mark.

"That doesn't mean I don't like to read fiction books – or that I can't," said Kevin.

"You are a weird duck," said Mark.

"Coming from the king of quacks," Kevin shot back.

Both boys stopped talking as they reached the spot where Adam and Jimmy waited.

"Now that you two made it, listen up. We have to run across fast and then leave some time between each person. Jimmy, how about you go first?" said Adam.

"Sure," said Jimmy. He looked forward and concentrated, taking in a few deep breaths before launching into a run. Jimmy didn't stop until he hit the wall on the other side. He turned and gave a thumbs up to the others.

"Ok. Who's next?" asked Adam.

"Me," said Mark. "Farmboy here is too slow anyway." He gave the insult and burst into a run toward Jimmy, bouncing off the wall on the other side.

Kevin was fuming as Adam held him back long enough to be safe. Mark had moved out of the way as if he knew that Kevin would run him over if he were anywhere near Kevin's path.

"Go," said Adam.

Kevin sprang into a fast sprint, much quicker than any of them thought the big guy could run. He stopped so fast at the wall on the other side that he only put his hands up to touch it lightly before turning toward Mark.

"See, my plan worked," said Mark as Kevin advanced on him. "I got you mad and you ran faster than you ever have before. I was just looking out for you. Keeping you safe." He kept talking as he backed away from Kevin.

"Keep talking like that and I'm going to call you Jimmy, Creampuff," said Kevin, his face breaking from a scowl to a wide grin. He had scared Mark and that was enough.

Adam decided enough time had gone by and he should get to the other side before anyone got into trouble, so he ran across the bridge too. He couldn't stop as gracefully as Kevin had, but he didn't smash into the wall either.

"We all survived," he said to the others.

Mark snorted. "Weren't we supposed to?"

Adam shrugged then chuckled.

"Stay there and let me check this area out before you go anywhere," he said, and began feeling the wall in front of him. Again, he worked his way to the single doorway in the middle of the wall, where he triggered another instruction telling him to walk through the door. It was exactly as he remembered. So far, none of the instructions had changed, except for the hole on the landing.

Instead of going through the door, he moved to the other side, triggered the same instructions again, and continued on until he met the wall to the far left. He checked the wall all the way to the edge of the cavern and found nothing.

"It's all clear," said Adam.

"Can I look over the edge?" asked Mark.

"Go for it," replied Adam.

Mark shuffled to the edge and looked down. Kevin and Jimmy joined him.

"That's just crazy," said Mark. "You can see a couple of feet down and then nothing."

"It's like the stairway," said Jimmy.

"Not something I want to check out too close," said Mark as he started to step backwards.

"Are you sure?" asked Kevin. He grabbed Mark by the shoulders and gave him a little shove in the direction of the cavern, but held him so he wouldn't really fall.

Mark screamed. Not just any scream, but the scream of someone in mortal danger. Instead of making the other boys laugh at him, it made them ashamed.

"Whoa," said Kevin. "Sorry man, I was just messing with you."

Mark looked hurt, but then he looked at Kevin and saw how sincere he was. "It's ok, man," was all he said, and they were ok with each other again.

"I think a hug is in order," said Jimmy.

"You want us to hug you?" asked Mark.

"No..." stammered Jimmy.

"I think he's scared. That's why he needs a hug," said Kevin.

"Yep. I'd agree," said Mark.

Jimmy tried to get a word in but was cut off.

"I forgot to bring his diapers, though. Does little Jimmy have to wee wee?" asked Mark.

Kevin and Mark started laughing as Jimmy smiled and brushed off the comments. "You're both such comedians," he said. He turned to Adam, "Let's get going before Cheech and Chong here get started again."

Adam nodded. "The next part is the long narrow hallway that comes out into the long staircase. It's probably still full of that water you can breathe. Once we're in the water I'll give you instructions."

With that, he turned and walked through the doorway.

CHAPTER SIXTEEN

The long hallway seemed tighter than it had the previous year. Maybe it was because Adam had grown over the last year, or maybe it was just the way memory usually works. Either way, it was still a more confining space than it had been and it was longer than he had remembered.

During the walk, Adam mentally prepared himself for dealing with the water. It hadn't been his favourite thing to do, but he managed. He was worried how the other three would deal with it, though. They hadn't dealt with the darkness in the stairway all that well, and to him that was minor. The water was a whole other level. It was so against everything a person had been taught about water, even in 14 short years.

To prepare, he remembered the first time he climbed back out of the water and had a coughing fit as soon as he tried to breathe. Larix had 'forgotten' to mention that it was easier if you exhaled as much water as possible from your lungs before you brought in fresh air. The second time, Adam had remembered to exhale hard and it went much better.

He reached the end of the hallway and looked down the long staircase. To his surprise the entire room was dry. Having learned his lesson at the beginning of that night's adventure, Adam waited until his friends stopped behind him before doing anything.

"Isn't there supposed to be water down there?" asked Mark.

"There was when I saw it last," said Adam.

"Where is it then?" asked Mark.

"I don't know," answered Adam. His thoughts raced through options and soon settled on a couple of answers.

"Either someone pumped it out or someone re-set the trap."

They thought about those two options for a while.

"If we go in there and set off the trap again, we can get out once the water rises to the top, right? That's how you got out the last time," said Kevin.

"Yeah, true. You see that hole in the wall, about halfway up?" Adam pointed at the wall far ahead. "That's where I came out. The water was only a couple of feet below that, so I dived in."

"I don't swim all that great," said Mark.

"You don't have to worry. This water makes you float a lot more than normal water."

"So how do you swim down? Don't you just keep floating to the top?" asked Mark.

"You float until you replace the air in your lungs with water, then you feel like you're swimming normally, just that you don't have to come up for air."

"Oh, ok," said Mark. "I'm willing to give it a try."

The others were surprised by his willingness.

"Let's do it, then," said Jimmy pointing the way down.

Adam nodded and began the descent.

He remembered the stairs from the first time, but not how scary they were. They were a few feet wide, dropping off into blackness on either side. Because there was no railing, it was very unnerving.

"Sorry Kevin, but I have to say that these stairs remind me of the scene in Lord of the Rings where they are running through the mines. The stairs were a lot like this. When I saw the movie I said I'd freak out if I was ever on stairs like those," said Mark.

"And how's it going so far?" asked Kevin.

"You just stay in front of me so I'll have something soft to land on and I'll be ok," said Mark, but he wasn't too convincing. The waver in his voice said otherwise.

"A step at a time is all we need, and we're not in a rush," said Adam.

"What time is it anyway?" asked Jimmy.

"Not a clue," said Adam, "but I'm not checking now."

Step after step they made their way down and as soon as they reached the bottom they turned to look up again.

"You said it was a long staircase last year, but that is an understatement," said Jimmy.

Adam nodded. "Amazing how things don't seem as bad when you have other things on your mind – like dying."

"Good point," said Jimmy.

"Let's stick close together in the next part. Once we go through the door there's a trigger and boulders block this door. I don't want anyone getting squished."

With that, he began walking into the next room. He made sure they stuck together, but as soon as he was into the 'V' shaped room, something seemed different. There were no stones blocking the way ahead. The tunnel he had to swim through and then up was unblocked. Before he did anything else, he made sure everyone was in the room and stopped, filling them in about his concern.

"Just keep going, I guess," said Kevin. The others agreed.

Adam nodded back. He took the next few steps slow until he heard a familiar click, just like the first time. Unlike the first time, nothing followed the click. He stopped and waited for a moment, then lifted his foot and set it down on the same spot again triggering the same clicking noise. Nothing happened.

"Looks like they pumped the water out," said Adam. "Let's keep going."

"I'm ok with that," replied Mark.

The others stayed quiet as they craned their necks taking in the entire room.

"How high was the water in here?" asked Jimmy.

Adam looked up, found the landing near the top and pointed at it.

"See that little bit of rock near the top? Just below there," he said.

Jimmy didn't reply but stared at the landing.

Adam continued down the hallway ahead. Again it seemed tighter and longer than he had remembered.

"Didn't you say you had to swim up at the end of this hallway?" asked Kevin.

Adam thought back again and remembered the previous year. "I saw rungs on the far wall as I swam, so we should still be able to climb up."

Once he reached the end of the hallway it turned upward. This time, his memory was exactly right and the ladder rungs were jutting out from the wall in front of him. He looked up and almost felt dizzy as he tried to judge the height.

"Who wants to go first?" asked Adam.

"Go right ahead," said Jimmy. "We'll follow behind, but not too close."

Adam hung his head. "Are you sure?" The look on the faces of the others gave him his answer. He sighed as he turned and grabbed the first rung giving it a hard tug to make sure it would hold him. It didn't budge so he began the long climb.

Climbing a ladder onto a single story house wasn't the scariest thing Adam ever did, but climbing up to the second story of his house to clean the gutters every year wasn't something he looked forward to. He knew it had to be done, but otherwise he was more than happy to stay on the ground. This climb was a lot higher than the second story eaves, though. The only way he could keep going was to not look anywhere but up to the next rung. If he looked too high he feared he would get dizzy, and looking down was totally out of the question. Rung after rung he pulled himself up, not bothering to count because he didn't want to know.

"How's it going up there?" asked Kevin from below.

Adam cleared his throat, hoping his friends didn't hear his fear. "Good," he managed to say, and he didn't think it sounded like the huge lie it was.

"I'm going to start now," said Kevin.

"Alright," Adam replied, but this time he knew he heard some fear.

He began to wish that the whole place had still been flooded, because breathing underwater, now that he had done it before, was way less scary than that climb. It was much easier to swim up to the top than it was to pull himself up rung by rung.

"Better pick up the pace," said Kevin from below. He seemed to be catching up.

"Yeah, yeah," Adam replied. His comment was loaded with sarcasm, but he was secretly glad. Kevin's voice had snapped him out of his trance of fear, so he began climbing again.

It seemed like forever and yet not very long at all, but once Adam reached the top he found a handhold in the floor and scrambled out. He felt like kissing the floor, but instead he lay on his back and breathed deeply a few times. He knew he didn't have a lot of time before Kevin showed up, and he didn't want to be seen lying around in that way.

After a few more puffs of air, Adam stood and looked around. That cave was exactly as he remembered it too. The landing he was on led to another deep cavern, and in the middle of the cavern was an island. On the island stood the pillar he would have to get the Impression Stone to land on in order to bring up the bridge.

Kevin grunted as he pulled himself up. "Jimmy's not too far behind me," he said as he stood and brushed himself off. As he straightened, he looked around wide-eyed.

Both boys said nothing until Jimmy poked his head out of the hole. Kevin walked over and gave him a hand, half-pulling him out onto the landing.

"Thanks," said Jimmy. "That really sucked." He looked back down the hole and then back to Kevin. "Mark hasn't even started yet." He rolled his eyes.

Kevin nodded and looked down the hole too. "Hey Creampuff, you coming?"

Mark stepped into view and looked back up at Kevin. "Not on your life, Farmboy."

"Why not?"

"Isn't it you that always says I need an elevator in my house because I am too lazy to take the stairs? Well, this is a lot higher than those stairs," said Mark, happy to use his own laziness as an excuse.

Kevin looked at Jimmy. In a low voice he said, "It's probably for the best. I wasn't sure *I* could make that climb myself," to which Jimmy nodded.

"You just stay there and don't move," yelled Jimmy down the hole. "I don't want you attracting any of the huge spiders or other animals that probably live here."

Jimmy pulled away from the hole and chuckled, then spoke quietly to Kevin. "He may not have to make the climb, but I don't want him to be too comfortable down there."

Kevin smiled back as they heard Mark saying, "You're just kidding, right? Guys?...Guys?"

They turned to face Adam.

"You're evil," said Adam, grinning wide, "but I like it."

Jimmy took a second to look around. "Whoa. This place is crazy."

"You had to land the Impression Stone on that little pillar over there?" asked Kevin.

Adam nodded. "And, it had to land in a small hole on top of the pillar."

Kevin had wandered toward the edge of the cavern. As soon as he got too close, flames shot up around the island. Kevin jumped back and they stopped.

"Whoa," he yelled as he jumped.

Adam grinned. "I forgot to remind you about that. Sorry."

Kevin nodded as if to say 'that's ok'.

"You guys just stand still. I want to check things out before we get into trouble."

The others nodded as Adam began searching. He hadn't felt the walls the first time he had ever been in the cave because of everything else going on at the time. He wasn't going to take a chance though, so he felt each surface he could.

When he was satisfied, he walked back to the others.

"I guess I should get out the Impression Stones and start throwing," he said. "Which one do you think I should try first, the new one or the old one? I've been wondering if the new one from Killaly does something different in here."

Jimmy spoke first, as if he had been thinking the same thing. "I would say use the old one. Even though you are already connected with the one from Killaly, you haven't thrown it to know if it will come back to you for sure. You might lose it."

Adam considered what Jimmy said. "I didn't know if the other one came back until I threw it either, but you have a good point. I'm going to try something first this time."

Adam reached in his pocket and pulled out the two stones. He selected the one from Killaly and put the other one back in his pocket before stepping over to the wall and setting it on the floor. He walked back to his friends again.

"What are you doing?" asked Jimmy.

"He's testing your theory," said Kevin.

Adam nodded. He concentrated on the Impression Stone and motioned for it to come back to him. He remembered that, if it worked, he didn't need to pull too hard or it would shoot back at him like a small bullet. The Impression Stone hopped to life and flew into his hand.

"That's just cool," said Jimmy. Kevin agreed.

"I think I'm going to start with this one," said Adam.

He walked to the edge of the cavern and when the flames began to shoot up he took a step backwards, shutting them off again. Since he had just tested the connection, he didn't have to go through that process again - just throw. His throw went wide by a few feet, but because of the practice and experience he'd had over the past year, he steered it down onto the pillar on the first try. Jimmy and Kevin were quite impressed.

"Isn't the pillar supposed to do something now?" asked Jimmy.

Adam waved his hand slightly and the Impression Stone shuffled along the top of the pillar until it fell into a hole. A loud click sounded throughout the cave, followed by the sound of gears turning. The pillar rose slowly upward. At the same time a bridge rose from the darkness and positioned itself so they could walk over to the island.

"This is like playing a live-action version of Tomb Raider. Sadly, McTaggart – you're no Lara Croft," said Jimmy.

Kevin chuckled, but Adam only smiled. He was too concentrated on the task ahead of him.

"Do we all go over or should one of us stay?" asked Kevin.

Jimmy answered, "We've come this far. Let's not stop here. Adam got back last time. We'll get back ok."

With that, they took their time and followed Adam across the bridge once he had made sure it was safe.

They stood around the pillar and looked at it.

"What next?" asked Jimmy.

Adam pulled the lapel pin from his pocket and placed it in the proper spot on top of the pillar. It dropped slowly into the island, and again the bridge fell away to be replaced by flame all around.

"Now that's freaky," said Jimmy.

"Thankfully the flames gave me cover last time," said Adam as they watched the pillar sink.

Soon the pillar had retreated into the island in the same way as Adam had remembered, but when he looked into the hole, it seemed different somehow.

He bent to get a better look. Right away he saw why it was different. The pillar had retracted further into the island. Adam was sure that the spot where he had found the fake Heartstone the previous year was near the top, but when he looked inside there was no opening at that spot. Another opening appeared six inches lower down. Something else caught his eye in that opening and his pulse quickened.

In it sat another bag - identical to the one he found the year before.

CHAPTER SEVENTEEN

"Is that a bag down there?" asked Kevin.

Adam's heart raced. What if it *was* the Heartstone, here all the time? He nodded back at Kevin and reached down to get it. As he did, another instruction triggered in his mind. It was exactly the same one as the year before, "Connect with the stone in the bag," was all it said.

Adam grabbed the bag and pulled it out. As he stood, Jimmy and Kevin crowded around for a look.

"I just had the same instruction as last year. It told me to connect with the stone in the bag – but if this is the real Heartstone, I'm not too sure I want to try."

They looked from Adam to the bag in his hand. "Well, there's only one way to find out, plus the instructions told you to do it. So far they haven't steered you wrong," said Jimmy.

Adam untied the knot on the drawstring and opened the mouth of the bag. He reached in and pulled a stone out. It looked identical to the fake Heartstone he found the previous year.

"How do we know if it's the real one or not?" asked Jimmy.

Adam shrugged. "I guess I have to connect with it," he said.

"But what if it *is* the real one?" asked Kevin. "What'll happen?"

"I don't know," said Adam. "If I don't come out of it, knock it out of my hands, ok?"

Kevin nodded. "Good luck."

Adam cupped the stone in his hands and brought it to his forehead, but was nervous to start. He took a deep breath and concentrated on making a connection.

Into the stone he fell, and he remembered the same sensation he had with the other Heartstone copy. He reached the center and again floated limbless inside. A small scroll came forward, filled with writing. Once it was close enough, Adam read:

To whoever is connected with this stone: this is not the Heartstone you are looking for, it is a copy. The real Heartstone has been taken away without the knowledge of Elianora or any others in the Sentinel League, in the hopes of keeping it safe.

We know our locations have been compromised. Elianora was unwilling to believe, so we have taken over.

The Aeturnum symbol appeared at the bottom of the scroll before Adam was thrown back to reality.

"Is it the real one?" asked Jimmy.

Adam shook his head. "And it had exactly the same message as the other one."

"Exactly?" asked Jimmy.

"Yep, right down to the Aeturnum symbol at the end," said Adam.

"Wow. That sucks," said Jimmy.

All were quiet for a while. Adam's mind was on fire, running through scenarios from the past, but nothing clicked. *Why would there be two fake Heartstones with the exact same message in them?* he wondered.

"Maybe Karl would understand. He's been in the League longer than us," said Kevin.

"Hopefully," said Adam. "I guess we'll find out tomorrow."

"Well, we might as well head back. I'm probably close to grounded already anyway," said Jimmy.

"It's only 10:37," said Adam, looking at his watch. "We've got lots of time."

He pocketed the second fake Heartstone.

"Let's go then," said Kevin as he led the way to the hole.

"We're done," he yelled down the hole.

"Hurry up," came Mark's voice from far below and out of sight.

"Why don't you wait at the bottom in case one of us falls?" asked Kevin.

"Sorry, I can't hear you," said Mark, his voice trailing off as the sentence ended. He had walked further into the hallway.

Kevin swung himself down into the hole and started descending. Jimmy had a little more trouble starting, but Adam had the most trouble of all. He sat with his legs dangling into the hole, then found a rung and spun around while holding the notch in the floor. Carefully, he took the first step, and then the second. After the fifth step he found a slow but steady rhythm and maintained it all the way to the bottom. On the way, he kept his mind on the message in the second fake Heartstone, which helped a lot, and soon he touched the ground.

When he turned to look where the others had gone, his heart sank. Ben Casey was staring straight at him, a shotgun held in his hands. He was pointing at the ground and not at anyone in particular. Just behind Ben, Mark, Jimmy and Kevin sat on the ground.

"Hello Sunshine," said Ben in his gravelly voice. "Thanks for joining us. Now we can have a little discussion."

Ben waved the barrel of the gun indicating that Adam should come toward him and sit with his friends.

"Thank you boys for waiting so quiet like I asked," Ben said to the others as Adam sat next to them. "Didn't want to scare you and have you fall."

His face didn't show concern.

"I should'a known it would be you guys again," he said. "In case you're wondering, I rigged an alarm on the office building. As soon as you opened it I headed out here. So why are you interrupting my evening and making me come all the way out here just to find you sneaking around?"

None of the boys offered a reason. Each was excited and scared to be facing Ben with a gun, alone in a very secret place. If Ben wanted to kill them, this would be a great location to do it. He could drop them into one of the caverns, never to be seen again.

"Speak up," yelled Ben, startling the boys, but they were still too nervous to speak.

"Well," began Jimmy, but he was cut off.

"I don't want to hear anything out of you, Lollipop. Half of what you say is a lie and the other half I don't trust. Creampuff," Ben pointed his gun at Mark, "speak."

Mark was clearly scared and it sounded in his voice as he stammered trying to get it to start working. "W...w...we j...just c...came here to see the place. W...we heard so much about it over the last year, so w...we convinced Adam to show it to us."

Adam thought Mark had come up with a pretty believable story, but the look on Ben's face stayed in its usual grumpy scowl.

"But *you* didn't go up there," said Ben pointing.

Mark shook his head. "Have you seen how high that is? No thanks."

Ben's face looked like it almost broke into a grin.

Almost.

"Did you get a good look?" Ben asked Kevin.

"Yep. It's pretty impressive," said Kevin in reply.

"You too Lollipop?"

Jimmy only nodded.

Ben stared at them for a few more long moments before coming back to Adam.

"You find what you were looking for?" he asked.

Adam felt his stare as if Ben were reading his mind.

"Just showing this place to the guys," he replied trying to be as calm as he could.

Ben continued to stare at him.

"Next time you want to come out here and poke around, tell me first so I don't run out here for no reason.

This stuff is a real pain to get off," he pointed at his underarms where black patches of something were smeared. Adam remembered Mark and Jimmy telling him about how Ben had used the sealant last year to become completely silent as he moved.

"Got it?" asked Ben.

They all nodded.

"Now get out."

They hopped to their feet and started moving at a fast walk with Ben close behind.

"What happened to all the water," asked Adam.

"We pumped it out," said Ben. "Didn't help that Larix had no more fear of the water, so might as well not have it in here 'til they decide what to do with this place."

Adam thought about it as they stepped out of the 'v' shaped room and began the long climb up the staircase.

"You guys ever think about railings?" asked Mark.

"This ain't the kinda place occupational safety comes to inspect ya know," replied Ben with a chuckle.

Adam could feel his leg muscles burn as they reached the halfway point. Going down was much easier than up, and the last time he went up these stairs he started at the halfway point where the water level met them. *Mark must be struggling*, he thought, and soon he knew he was right.

"Break time," called Mark as he sat down on the step directly in front of Kevin. Kevin nearly toppled over Mark because of how fast Mark sat down.

"You trying to kill me?" Kevin cried out as he caught his balance with the help of Jimmy.

Mark looked sheepish. "Sorry. I just need a break."

"I knew you weren't in great condition, but I didn't think you were in that bad of shape, Creampuff," said Ben, barely breathing heavy and seeming full of energy.

"How can an old guy like you not be tired from these stairs?" asked Mark.

Ben grunted. "Just 'cause I'm a little fat don't mean I'm outta shape. I work out everyday, just not the same way as everyone else. I might have to whip you into shape," he said, then looked straight at Adam. "If you live that long," he finished after a pause. A moment later he chuckled, and it sent shivers up Adam's spine.

"Ok, let's keep moving," said Kevin. "Just go a little slower this time. We're not in a huge panic."

Normally Mark would have refused or complained, but since he felt the 'if you live that long' comment was directed at him, his adrenaline got him up and moving right away.

A few minutes later they were through the long, narrow hallway and standing on the landing before the big cavern.

"Break time," called Mark again and he flopped on the floor, sweat pouring from his forehead. The other boys sat near him but Ben stayed standing, grumbling something that sounded a lot like, "Lazy kids."

After a minute of rest they moved toward the bridge. Thankfully it was visible from that side of the cavern. Before anyone could say anything, Ben dashed across to the other side silent as could be.

"Who's following?" asked Adam.

"I'm not going first but I'll go second," said Mark. "I don't want to be alone with that guy." He nodded at Ben.

Kevin shook his head. "I'll go," he said. He looked up the bridge, breathed deep and launched into a run. In no time he was over.

Mark was true to his word and ran as fast as he could, but with all of the exercise he had so far, he wasn't all that fast. The trapdoor opened as he had most of his weight on the other side, but it tripped him up enough that he fell and rolled down the bridge. He stopped with one arm and one leg dangling over the edge into darkness. As soon as he realized how close he was to going over, he rolled away from the edge until he hit the wall. Seconds later he composed himself and stood, walking the rest of the way down.

Adam and Jimmy looked at each other, eyes wide.

"After you," said Jimmy, pointing at the bridge. "I want to make sure Mark didn't break it on the way over."

"Thanks," said Adam. He rolled his eyes and looked at the bridge. He could see the trapdoor had reset, so he prepared himself and took off running. He ran with all the speed he could muster, determined not to get tripped up like Mark, and he ran smoothly to the other side. A few moments later Jimmy joined them.

"You alright?" Adam asked Mark. "That was quite the tumble."

Mark nodded, trying to look tough. "No problem. It wasn't that bad."

Adam didn't buy it and neither did anyone else, but they let it slide.

"Now we go up one more set of stairs," said Adam, "and remember, stay on the left side now."

Suddenly, Adam had a thought.

"How did you know which side the hole was on?" he asked Ben.

"I found the edge of the landing, put my foot down and checked, how else?" replied Ben like it was the simplest logic in the world.

"I mean, it changed sides since last year, didn't it?"

Ben nodded. "It changes every day at around midnight." He said it as if Adam should have known that little detail.

"Ok then," was all Adam could reply. "Off we go."

He led the way into the darkness. Step after step moved past, and this time he counted. Fifty, Fifty-one, fifty-two... Each step was tested for a millisecond before he committed to it, afraid of making a mistake.

At step sixty he paused and called back behind him, "How's it going guys?"

"Good," came the reply from three young voices, followed by a grunt further down.

"I'm at the sixtieth step. See you at the landing. Well, not really," he said as he re-thought his statement. They wouldn't actually *see* each other until they reached the top.

The pace he kept was half that of the ascent up the long staircase, partly due to fatigue and partly because it was a blind climb. At 140 steps he made it to the landing. Immediately he let the others know and continued climbing.

"At the landing," called Kevin.

"Made it," called Jimmy a few moments later.

"I'm here," called Mark through great puffs. "Ben's right behind me."

"See you at the top," Adam called back down as he continued upward.

The moment he broke out into the starlight sky he took a deep breath of the crisp country air. Even though it had a hint of the cows nearby and a skunk some way off, it smelled better than the stale air in the caves.

In short order Kevin and Jimmy came up too, and a few minutes later Mark and Ben arrived.

Ben didn't look like he had done any work whatsoever. Mark looked like he had just finished a marathon.

"Let's close this up and go home," said Ben, looking to Adam.

Adam looked back and shrugged. He had only ever *opened* the staircase before.

"Just grab the side of the office and pull down until it clicks into place."

Adam did as he was told. The building pivoted into place easily.

"And she said you were smart," said Ben with a mean laugh.

"We better head for home if we want to make it before 11:30," said Adam after looking at his watch. He hadn't realized how much time it took to get back out of the caves.

"I see you guys rode your bikes. I guess I could give you a ride in my truck," said Ben.

Adam was surprised by the offer.

"Sure," said Mark before anyone could say otherwise.

Jimmy looked around. "Where is it?"

"I parked it a little up the back road. Wait here and I'll come get you."

Ben jogged off toward his truck.

As soon as he was out of earshot, the boys huddled together.

"He suspects that I found something while we were down there. Take these," said Adam as he emptied his pockets and gave everything to Kevin.

Kevin looked surprised, but stuffed it all in his pockets.

Ben's truck roared to life in the distance. Shortly, it pulled into the yard. It was an older regular cab Ford in pristine condition. The boys loaded their bikes, careful not to scratch the paint.

"You three ride in the back. Sunshine is riding up front with me," said Ben.

Adam gulped.

The others climbed carefully into the back of the truck while Adam slid in the side door. As was expected, the interior was spotless. Everything shone like brand new under the glare of the interior light.

Ben slid into the driver's seat and put the truck in gear, backing it up and heading toward the back road.

After they made it to the monitoring station, Ben began to speak.

"So, Sunshine, did you find the Heartstone?" asked Ben matter-of-fact.

It was so direct that it shocked Adam.

"No," he replied. It wasn't a lie. He hadn't found the Heartstone.

Even though he was driving, Ben glared at Adam long enough that Adam panicked and pointed at the road.

Ben was silent until they turned toward town and had driven a little way.

"If you do find it, you bring it to me right away, ok? It's my job to take care of it."

The way Ben said 'take care of it' made Adam's gut tighten.

"If you *don't* bring it to me, I can't help it if you get hurt," he continued.

Adam nodded, but every part of him was crying 'get me out of here'.

Minutes later, they pulled up in Ben's driveway and the boys climbed out of the back. Before Adam could get out of the cab, Ben grabbed his arm hard.

"Don't forget, I don't want anything bad to happen to you or your friends, so if you find out anything you should probably tell me right away, got it?"

Adam nodded again. "Will do," was all he managed to say before Ben let him go.

He pulled the handle and slid out of the truck as smooth as he could, although he was mentally rattled by Ben's words.

The others had all of the bikes unloaded by the time Adam got to the back. Ben followed and stood right next to Adam, making him even more uncomfortable.

He ruffled Adam's hair and said, "Be good."

Adam got on his bike as fast as he could and waved a weak goodbye to Ben, then followed the others as they coasted over to Mark's driveway.

Mark parked his bike beside the garage and walked back to the boys.

"He went inside," said Mark as he looked over Adam's shoulder.

Adam quickly recounted everything Ben had said.

"He sounds like a mobster," said Mark.

"Still, I don't think my parents will believe he's guilty," said Kevin. "We'd have to catch him in the act of doing something wrong."

"Just like Karl said," said Adam. "If Karl can help us figure out these stones tomorrow, maybe we can find the Heartstone and set a trap for Ben."

The other boys agreed.

"I'm sleeping in and then I have to watch my sisters tomorrow afternoon, so I won't be able to see you until after supper," said Mark.

Jimmy nodded. "I forgot that we're going shopping for clothes tomorrow. I won't be home until after supper either," he said.

"I don't know what Dad has planned for me," said Kevin, "but I'll come over as soon as I can. You guys find us as soon as you're free, ok?"

Jimmy and Mark nodded.

"When are we going to talk to Karl?" asked Kevin.

"He doesn't get back until tomorrow afternoon," said Adam. "Should we go see him when we're all available?"

"Yeah. I want to be there," said Jimmy.

"Ok, I'll wait until we can all go see him together," said Adam.

"I have to get home pretty quick," said Jimmy after glancing at his watch.

Adam and Kevin followed Jimmy as Mark went into his house. A few minutes later, Kevin and Adam had dropped off Jimmy and stopped at the intersection where they would have go separate directions.

"Hang on," said Kevin as he stuck his hand in his pocket. He held out the Impression Stones, the fake Heartstone and the lapel pin.

"Actually, why don't you keep them tonight?" asked Adam. "It would make me feel much better."

Kevin considered it for a moment. "Are you sure?"

Adam nodded. "I think it's the safest. Only the two of us will know you have them, and we both know my house is a huge target now."

Kevin nodded. "Ok, then. I'll hide them good."

"Thanks," said Adam.

"See ya," said Kevin as he turned his bike for home.

"See ya," echoed Adam doing the same.

CHAPTER EIGHTEEN

For once Adam slept in. Usually he was up by 7 am, but that morning he had slept until 8:30. It must have been all of the exercise and excitement from the previous evening that tired him out again, he thought. He then remembered the morning after a similar day the previous year when Kevin had brought him a 'coffee', although it seemed so long ago. Still, the memory made him smile as he lay there.

It was going to be another beautiful day, so Adam was sure Kevin wouldn't be able to get away until after supper. That was ok; it felt like a good day to be lazy. Another thought struck Adam. He had slept in long enough that Mary would be gone to work. Just that thought alone made him spring out of bed, throw on some clothes and tramp down the stairs to find something to eat.

After a breakfast of stale rye bread and butter chased down with some water, Adam sat down in the living room and turned on the TV. Local morning TV shows were terrible, but they were easy on the mind. He could understand how Mark enjoyed watching TV so much, especially since he had so many channels to choose from compared to Adam.

A couple of wasted hours later, Adam's belly told him it was time to eat again. Sometimes Mary would come home for lunch, but more often than not she would make something at work, so Adam didn't worry about preparing anything for her.

In the end, Adam made some noodle soup, the cheap kind with nothing but Chinese writing on it. One of the pictures looked somewhat like a chicken, so he took the chance on it and he was right. It wasn't great, but it filled his belly, especially when he ate another piece of stale rye bread alongside.

It was 12:30 when he decided to head out to his garage. He hadn't thought about it until he was seated at his table, but having given Kevin almost everything for the evening had lifted a great weight from his shoulders. Until then, he didn't realize that it was affecting his ability to get a good night of sleep.

He still had the box Elianora gave him, and it still contained the first fake Heartstone. It was hidden in a new spot in the rafters that he had noticed while tarring the front roofline.

That was when he remembered his connection with the second fake Heartstone. What did it mean? Why have two fake Heartstones? And on top of that, why have the identical message in each one? It made no sense to Adam at all. He had expected to find the real Heartstone in the second location, and when it wasn't the actual Heartstone, he expected to get a clue about where it had gone.

His mind raced over possibilities, but each one seemed to get more unreasonable than the last. Finally he shook his head and looked for something else to occupy his mind.

As he looked around the room, he heard heavy footsteps in the alley behind the garage. A figure swept past the small side window and knocked on the garage door.

Adam walked over and opened the door.

"Hi Karl," said Adam. "We were going to come and see you after supper."

Karl nodded. "I just couldn't wait to hear how it went yesterday, so I came over as soon as I got home. Are your friends coming over soon?"

"No. They all have things to do this afternoon. That's why we were going to find you later."

"Oh, ok. Do you think they will mind if you tell me now what happened? I have to go see a client after supper."

Adam thought about it for a moment. He was sure the others would rather have Karl's opinion sooner than having to wait another night, so he invited Karl in and told him all that had happened, emphasizing all that Ben had said.

Karl looked shocked. "I knew it," he said, nodding his head. "Do you have the fake Heartstones?" he asked.

"No. I hid everything somewhere else just in case someone felt like breaking in here again."

Karl nodded. "That was a good idea. Can you get them without being noticed and meet me at my house?"

"I think so."

"Good. I don't have much time, so bring them over as soon as you can. I did some research and think I can shed some light on them and everything that's going on as soon as you get there," said Karl. He stood and made for the door.

"Do you like brownies?" he asked, turning back to Adam.

Adam thought it was strange that Karl was thinking about food, but looked at the size of him and the feeling passed.

Adam nodded.

"Good. I always think better when I'm snacking on brownies. I'll pull some out of the freezer for us to eat while we figure this all out."

Karl opened the door and walked away.

Adam waited until Karl was gone for a few minutes, hopped on his bike and pedaled for Kevin's house. In no time at all he was pulling into the long driveway.

Kevin was cutting the lawn using the riding lawn mower. Headphones covered his ears and he seemed to be shaking to the music and singing along until he noticed Adam. He stopped immediately and began to smile and blush a little.

Adam dropped his bike in the driveway and walked over to the lawn mower while Kevin shut it down and took off his headphones.

"Looks like you're having a rockin good time working," said Adam.

"Yeah yeah," replied Kevin. "What's up? I still have a bunch of stuff to do today, so I can't come over yet."

Adam frowned. "Too bad. Karl came over just now and he wants to talk about everything. He has to see a client tonight and would like to see the two fake Heartstones. He says he knows a few things about them, so I came to get them from you."

"Aw man, I'd like to be there. Oh well...c'mon, they're all in the shop," said Kevin as he led the way.

Kevin stepped into the shop and walked toward the back. He reached up and took down an old milk crate that sat on a high shelf, then pulled an old potato sack off of it. He picked up all of the items and handed them to Adam.

"Promise me you'll come get me right after supper and I'll be the first one you tell what happens at Karl's?" said Kevin.

"I promise," Adam agreed.

Kevin grabbed a plastic grocery bag from another shelf and had Adam place all of the items inside.

"It'll look less suspicious this way," he said.

"I appreciate it," said Adam. "My pockets were getting pretty full."

Kevin led Adam out of the shop and back to his bike. "I better get cutting or I won't get done before supper," he said. He gave Adam a wave and returned to the lawn mower.

Adam jumped on his bike and rode back home fast. He burst into his garage and grabbed the box Elianora had given him, since it still contained the other fake Heartstone. He put all of the items in the box, then placed the box back into the plastic bag.

Next, Adam jumped on his bike again and rode as fast as he could over to Karl's. He pulled his bike into the back yard and leaned it against the garage, then walked to the side door and rang the doorbell.

Karl opened the door and motioned for Adam to step inside.

"Just leave your shoes on and come to the table," said Karl.

The moment Adam stepped inside the door his nose was filled with the most amazing smell of chocolate.

"Is that your brownies?" he asked.

Karl nodded.

"They smell amazing," said Adam.

Karl smiled. "I *am* German, you know. We Germans are known for chocolate. I actually warmed the brownies in the oven for us. It's the proper way to eat them. Come come." Karl waved for Adam to step further inside.

Adam wandered into the house and pictured himself like a cartoon mouse floating though the air following the smell radiating from a block of cheese ahead. Sitting at the table were two large plates of brownies. Karl pointed to one of the chairs.

"You must have a glass of cold milk with that – it's the only way," he said.

Adam nodded as he sat. His stomach grumbled in anticipation.

"Don't worry about being polite, dig in," said Karl as he filled two glasses.

Adam didn't wait one more second. He devoured the top two pieces in no time. He slowed down to savour the flavour of the third and fourth. By the time he was starting the fifth piece, Karl had set a glass of milk down in front of him and began eating from his own plate.

"This is my mother's recipe. What do you think?"

Adam could only nod, roll his eyes and give Karl a thumbs up as he chewed, then chased it all down with a large swig of milk.

"So, show me these fake Heartstones," said Karl.

Adam handed the bag over and continued eating while Karl took out the box and opened it.

"I'm amazed that these are fake. They have so much detail," said Karl.

Adam was slowing down on his sixth piece. The sugar rush was starting to make him feel woozy, so he decided not to finish that piece and take a good long drink of milk. It helped a little, so he sat back and watched as Karl checked out the stones.

A crumb dropped to the table. Karl immediately picked it up and placed it on Adam's plate.

"Thanks," said Adam.

Karl returned to the stones, turning each one over in his hands, checking them closely.

"Do you mind if I try and connect with one?" he asked.

"Go ahead," said Adam.

He sat back and looked around, since he had seen Karl connect with stones many times before. He had never been inside Karl's house so his eyes wandered around. The kitchen was dated but spotlessly clean. Every item seemed to be lined up exactly with precision.

The kitchen and dining room opened into a large living room. Knickknacks lined shelves everywhere, all laser-straight. Even the bit of carpet he could see in the living room seemed to have been combed to perfection.

Karl slammed the stone down on the table. He looked frustrated and was saying words in German. From the way they were said, Adam guessed they were curses. It seemed out of character for Karl.

Karl looked directly at Adam.

That's when it hit him.

Adam tried to stand, but his legs had turned to jelly. He slid off the chair and hit the floor.

He had been drugged.

"I'm sorry, but it's the only way," said Karl.

Adam slipped off into the darkness. The last vision he remembered was of Karl standing over him, shaking his head back and forth.

CHAPTER NINETEEN

Adam dreamed he was struggling his way up a mountain of brownies, trying to make it to the top before the creature below him caught up. As he struggled to make it to the top, something grabbed his foot so he kicked his way free and struggled some more, but he just couldn't get any traction. Just when it seemed that he was getting away, the monster below him roared and a river of milk washed him off of the mountain and into the waiting mouth of the monster.

Just as the monster was about to bite down, Adam woke up. Right away he was startled by the fact that he couldn't sit up. In fact, he couldn't move much at all. About all he could do was open his eyes and look around. At least, he was pretty sure his eyes were open. He couldn't see anything, so either he had gone blind or his head was covered.

He wriggled his feet, but they seemed to be tied. He moved his hands but they seemed to be tied behind him too. He tried to open his mouth to say something, but found that it was taped shut. Shortly after, he gave up and just listened.

He was definitely in the back of a car and they were going somewhere. It was over a gravel road, that he knew for sure. That narrowed it down to a few thousand miles of roads in the surrounding area of Grayson.

A huge wave of drowsiness swept over him again, and soon he drifted back off to sleep once more. This time he had no dreams.

The next time he woke, he opened his eyes and had to close them again because of the bright light focused on his face.

"Where am I?" he asked in a drowsy voice, but heard no answer. At least he didn't have anything over his mouth anymore, he thought.

He squinted and tried to make out the room he was in, but he couldn't. It echoed in a strange way, like being inside a tin can that smelled faintly like old beer.

As he listened, he heard a voice talking somewhere nearby, although it was muffled.

"Yes. Yes, I have him and all of the items. I am just waiting for the transport." It was Karl speaking, unmistakable by his slight German accent.

"He needs to get here right away. An hour is too long."

"Ok...Ok...I understand! Just tell him to get here now!"

Footsteps approached. A thin metal door swung open and then closed.

"You're awake," said Karl in a voice that was as calm as if he hadn't just drugged and kidnapped Adam.

"Let me go!" yelled Adam at the top of his lungs. His drowsiness was wearing off.

Karl laughed. "Yell all you want. No one is going to hear you all the way out here," he said.

"Where are we?" asked Adam.

"We are a couple of miles outside of Killaly, actually. We use this location in case we needed to 'store' some things."

"Who is 'we'?" asked Adam. "You and Ben are working together?"

Karl laughed. "No no. I couldn't work with that buffoon. He has nothing to do with this. This was completely my plan from the beginning."

Adam's mind raced through scenes with Ben over the past few days. Nothing seemed to make sense. All signs pointed to Ben as having been involved.

"Don't get me wrong – Ben *is* dangerous and I don't prefer to be on his bad side, but he is also an idiot and easily fooled. I dropped clues that you were hiding information about the Heartstone's location and he did the rest himself."

"But I don't have any information," said Adam.

"You do, but you're too young and naive to know it."

Adam thought about it for a moment and his face showed his confusion.

Karl grinned and nodded. "Exactly. The answer is right in front of you, but you don't know it."

"Tell me then," said Adam.

"In good time," replied Karl. "You'll find out soon enough."

Adam struggled with the ropes, but they held tight.

"Easy now, you'll only tire yourself out some more. The drugs haven't worn off completely yet," said Karl.

"Can you at least get this light off my face?" asked Adam

"I suppose," said Karl and he turned the light to face the other direction.

Once Adam's eyes adjusted to the new level of light, he looked around. He was in the middle of a tall round building with grey, corrugated steel walls. He recognized it immediately. It was a grain bin. The only furnishings in the room were the chair he was sitting on and the table in front of him that the lamp stood on. Beside the lamp on the table was the small wooden box with a gold latch on the front that contained all of the items he had delivered right to Karl.

"Where did you get the power for the light?" asked Adam, realizing that grain bins didn't have power outlets inside.

"This is an abandoned farm yard, but the current owner has power nearby. The yard is heavily treed so no one can see anything from the road and there are no windows in here. It's a perfect location."

"So *you* broke into my house? What were you looking for?"

Karl nodded. "I went through all of the trouble to get your mom out of the house, not realizing you were going to be at the game. I gave her and Karen Garagan the tickets to the dinner theater. We all thought that the Heartstone was hidden in the statue of Brutus and it could only be opened by your dad's lapel pin, so I was going to get you to come along and open it. When I didn't find you, I searched your house for the pin until I found out that you were in Killaly and had already opened the statue. I was surprised to hear that you only found another Impression Stone, so I decided to let you try and figure out the rest on your own."

"Is that why you didn't look through my mom's room?"

Karl nodded.

Even though Adam's mind was racing, one point became clear about the time line.

"How did you know I had the Impression Stone so quickly?"

Karl grinned. "It pays to stay well connected. Knowledge is power."

Adam knew instantly who told Karl.

"Mayor Gunderson is in on it," said Adam.

Karl just shrugged and remained silent.

"Why are you doing this? Why didn't you just kill me at your house and take the fake Heartstones and my dad's pin?" asked Adam.

Karl frowned. "I may be some things, but I am no killer. Regardless of what you think, I like you in some ways. But to answer your question about killing you, you are worth more alive than dead. Larix has put a large bounty on you alive, and I intend to cash in on it, plus a couple of other things. I've spent too many years on the road selling insurance, listening to everyone else's problems. Now I'll be able to have a new life, far from here but in the lap of luxury."

"But why? You're high up in the League, isn't that enough?"

"No!" yelled Karl, his face turning dark purple with rage. "It is NOT enough! I have done everything they have asked of me for years on end, and what have they given me? Nothing! I was in line for the top job when your dad died. I was also a Number 3. And they gave it to Gurpreet instead of me. He can't connect with the Impression Stones either, so I don't understand why."

At that moment, Karl stopped speaking, realizing he had probably spoken too much.

"You can't connect with the Impression Stones? How is that possible? You're the best Kurler I've ever seen," said Adam, surprised.

Karl was quiet.

Adam thought about it for a moment. "Elianora was relying on you to get the Heartstone when she needed to move it after my Dad died, wasn't she?"

Karl grimaced. "Yes."

"I still can't believe you can't connect with the Impression Stones."

"Why, just because *you* can? I can't, ok. I don't know why. Everyone has always assumed that I could because of the way I Kurl. I can connect with them enough to throw them, but Elianora was worried that I would make a mistake in the caves and die trying to get through. Even when I asked to be given the ability, Elianora refused to give it to me."

Adam was confused. "She can *give* you the ability?"

Karl grinned an evil grin. "They don't like to tell you that little piece of information. I've learned that myself. She can do it but would never grant it to me. It was soon after she refused that I contacted Larix and told him where the Heartstone was. Until then I had only given him the locations where I had uncovered it had been in the past."

"You're the one who called him? You had him destroy Waldron and Langenburg? People *died* because of you!"

"Yes yes, but people die all the time and for a lot stupider reasons. You forget I have sold insurance for a lot of years. I don't have all that many years left, so when the opportunity presented itself I jumped on it."

"So is Larix on his way to kill me?" Adam gulped as he finished the sentence.

Karl shook his head. "No, he needs you first. He is sending his best man to take us to him. He will not risk being captured again. I am sure he will make an example out of you as soon as he can so that others don't stand in his way."

Adam wondered why Larix would need him anyway.

"How is Aeturnum involved in all of this?" asked Adam.

Karl shrugged. "Even I don't know all of those answers," he said, "But I am sure Larix does."

"So he hasn't let you in on everything then? Has he told John Gunderson?"

The comment made Karl angry. Adam watched as his face darkened. "I am lucky that he didn't send someone to kill me after you got him captured last year. It took a lot of convincing that I could be the one to deliver you to him along with clues to the location of the Heartstone. He even promised to pay me well if I could."

"Like he's good for his word," said Adam.

Karl got angrier. "What was I supposed to do? Let him kill me? He promised that he would share the secret of the deepest connections with me if I didn't fail this time. Then I can finally be the best Kurler who ever lived."

Adam sensed that Karl was trying to convince himself as much as Adam.

"So now we wait. His man will be here to escort us soon. By the time anyone knows you are missing, we'll be long gone."

CHAPTER TWENTY

Adam wished he had been able to look at his watch because the next stretch of time could have been ten minutes or two hours. Time ticked by as he thought about his friends at their homes. Kevin was probably still cutting the huge lawn in his yard. Jimmy was probably trying on clothes in the nearest city, Melville, and Mark was most likely sitting on the couch watching TV while Miri and Siri played around him. Each of them was comfortable in their homes while Adam sat there, tied up and fearing for his life.

Karl had left him alone in the grain bin and wandered far enough away that Adam couldn't hear him. It seemed like Karl wanted to get away instead of continuing their conversation, which was fine with Adam. There was enough he was trying to make sense of already.

How come he didn't figure out that Karl was the one who broke into his house, not Ben? He beat himself up mentally for the lapse in judgment. It was an error that looked like it would cost him dearly. Soon he would be gone to somewhere far away, probably to never see his friends again.

That's when he thought of his mom. Mary had never been all that much of a mother to him, after all, but in that moment of despair, Adam choked up when he thought that he might never see her again. He sniffled as his eyes started to glass over.

He closed his eyes tight and shook his head, determination returning. His mind kicked into gear again and raced through images and conversations. He was determined not to give up so easily.

What had Ben said once before? You *guys are pretty good at getting out of sticky situations?* Something like that. Whatever it was, it snapped Adam back into action. His mind raced as it thought of options.

He looked around and the only things he could see were the table, the lamp and the box that held all of his things. As he examined the box, he noticed that it had a snap latch that didn't look like it was secured.

He imagined the inside of the box and his mind's eye saw the two fake Heartstones, the lapel pin, and the two Impression Stones. While his mind saw, it also reasoned something that gave Adam hope.

Adam sat there concentrating and willed the Killaly Impression Stone to return to his hand. He moved his hand against the ropes that bound him. The box hopped as the stone hit the top and the latch popped open a little. He repeated the process one more time and the lid flipped open before the stone flew into his hand.

He felt the sharp edge sting as it landed in his hand, then he shifted it around until he could use the stone to cut the rope. His heart raced as he sawed, and little by little he made it through the rope. As it fell away, he heard Karl cough followed by footsteps growing louder.

He stood quickly and put the stone back in the box, closed the lid and sat down. He grabbed the rope and managed to make it look like it was still tied around his wrists while he held the two cut ends in his hands. The only thing Karl would notice is that Adam's hands were now in front instead of behind him, but there was no time to worry about that. Maybe he could surprise Karl and overpower him, but without the use of his legs, it wouldn't make much sense.

The door opened and Karl stepped inside. He was holding a shotgun and pointed it at Adam. Immediately he noticed Adam's hands. His face showed some anger, but calmed soon after. He obviously thought the ropes were still tied.

"I'll bet it wasn't too easy to get your hands out front now, was it?"

Adam shook his head. Karl laughed.

"At least I won't have to carry you anymore. Get up, we have to go."

Adam looked at Karl as if he didn't understand.

"You should be able to hop. Come on now, hop out to the car. The only way I'm carrying you now is if you have shotgun pellets in your legs." He pointed the gun at Adam's lap.

Adam stood as fast as he could.

"I knew you just needed a little motivation," said Karl.

"Come on out to the car now," he said as he backed out of the door.

Adam heard a car door open off to the right. As soon as he stuck his head outside, Karl pulled a hood over it.

"You remember this from last year?" he asked.

Adam nodded. His heart sunk and his gut tightened again.

"So you know not to struggle. It's an ugly thing to watch someone being choked into unconsciousness."

Karl took Adam under the arm and led him toward the car, helping him hop along. After helping him get inside, Karl told him to lie down and pull his feet in before he closed the door. A minute later the car rocked as Karl got in, and soon they were moving. It sounded as though he had set the small box on the passenger seat.

"Where are we going?" asked Adam.

"Not too far from here. You just wait."

The thought that it wasn't too far away did little to loosen the knot in his gut.

A few minutes later the car turned left, and not too far down another gravel road it slowed and turned right again before coming to a stop. Karl got out, again making the car rock violently.

"You've got him?" asked a muffled voice.

"In the back," said Karl.

"Get him out here so I can make sure," said the voice. It seemed familiar somehow.

A few crunches of gravel and the door opened. "Wait," said Karl. A moment later the ropes were falling from Adam's feet.

"Come out," said Karl.

Adam shuffled out, careful to keep a tight hold on the rope around his wrists. He had to make sure it still looked believable so he held his hands tight to his body. As soon as he was out, he let Karl lead him around.

"Here he is," said Karl.

"How do I know for sure? Take the hood off," said the familiar voice.

"Oh, sorry," replied Karl.

Adam felt hands circle his neck with the same strange motion Ben had used the previous year and suddenly there was bright light again. As Adam's eyes adjusted, he recognized the other man immediately. It was the guard that had hit Adam with his gun in the Radome caves the previous year.

"You," said Adam.

"You remember me," said the man.

"Believe me, I've tried to forget," said Adam.

The man smiled. Then he punched Adam hard in the chest.

"I've been waiting all year to do that. You got me in trouble with the boss."

Adam tried to catch his breath as he rolled around on the ground. The man's punch winded him. He had never been hit like that before.

As he rolled around he got a good look at where he was. It was a large empty clearing surrounded by thick trees, and near him in the middle Adam saw something that looked strange. It was a Radome like the one at Grayson, but less than half the size. Other than that, there was nothing else in the area.

"You got the other stuff?" asked the man.

"Yes, Butcher," said Karl. He shuffled around to the other side of the car and fetched the box.

After he handed it over, the guard opened it and looked inside.

"Good job. The boss is gonna be really happy with us," he said.

"So, how are we getting there?" asked Karl.

Adam watched as the man called 'Butcher' motioned his head to the Radome.

"I've never travelled that way before," said Karl, looking surprised. "Will it work for all of us?"

Butcher shrugged. "It's supposed to be enough." Then he sighed. "Anyway, the boss said that if you didn't come through on this job I was supposed to take you to him and he would torture you until you died. Since you didn't fail, I'm supposed to help you connect with the stones."

Karl gulped, "You can do that?"

"Yep. The boss showed me how."

Karl looked to get excited at the prospect. Adam had a bad taste creep into the back of his throat.

"Take out one of the stones from the box," said Butcher.

"Which one?" asked Karl.

"Any one," yelled Butcher.

Karl grabbed one of the fake Heartstones.

"Now connect with it."

Karl excitedly placed the stone between his hands and brought it up to his forehead.

"Now, concentrate as hard as you can," said Butcher.

Adam looked in horror as a glint of steel flashed in his eyes. By the time he could yell 'no', the knife was buried to the hilt in the middle of Karl's chest.

"The boss told me to tell you that now you're connected with the stones forever," said Butcher.

After Butcher withdrew the knife, Karl fell to his knees and looked at Adam. He mouthed the word 'sorry' and then keeled over.

Karl was dead.

CHAPTER TWENTY ONE

The scream hung on Adam's lips as he stared at Karl's lifeless body. It was the first time he had seen a person die in his life, and it would forever haunt him. Karl's eyes remained open, looking off into the distance as if he were watching a sunset, unblinking.

Butcher took the fake Heartstone from Karl's lifeless hand and then wiped the blood from his knife on Karl's shirt. He placed the stone back in the wooden box, snapping the clasp shut tight, then slipped the box in a holster on his belt.

That was when he looked at Adam. Fear and hate filled every molecule in Adam's body, but he didn't understand why he was angry. Karl *had* just betrayed him, after all.

"Why?" was all that Adam could ask.

"I saved him from a lot of torture in front of a lot of people," said Butcher as if he had done Karl a favour. "The boss was generous and spared him a humiliating death."

Adam was speechless. Spared him? *Lied* to him was more accurate.

"Time to go," said Butcher grabbing Adam under the arm and leading him toward the Radome.

Adam cleared his throat, and with a shaky voice asked, "How?"

Butcher pointed at the Radome.

Adam still looked confused.

"It's a transporter," he said as they walked. "Don't ask me how it works 'cause I don't know. I know it uses a bunch of energy. We need to get in there."

Adam did as Butcher said, leading the way to the Radome. As he approached, he noticed that it seemed to be almost glowing.

Adam's mind was in overdrive once again, running through scenarios of how he could possibly get out of this one. He was fast approaching the ladder leading up into the Radome and he would have to climb or get knifed. The power of Butcher's punch from earlier still ached in his chest and he knew he couldn't take another one.

As Adam reached the ladder he heard something whiz through the air. In a fraction of a second Butcher had blocked it with his own knife, knocking it to the ground. It was a knife like Butcher's, only much smaller.

"Butcher!" came a gravel throated yell from far away in the direction of the trees. It was quickly followed by two more knives.

Butcher strained to block the knives as Ben ran toward them. Next, he looked at Adam and then back to Ben. He clearly was torn – should he deal with Ben or get Adam into the Radome.

Butcher decided to go for Adam, but Adam saw it coming. Instead of standing still and waiting, he dropped the rope and dove to the side, rolling around the

Radome's center pillar and running out of the line of fire. Butcher missed Adam by a hair and instead had to block another knife thrown at him by Ben.

"Hey, old man," said Butcher, "why don't you go home before you get hurt?"

Ben laughed as he ran. "You couldn't beat me ten years ago. What makes you think you can now?"

Butcher readied himself to fight Ben when a van roared around the corner. It was Gurpreet!

Butcher quickly evaluated his chances of taking on multiple people at once and decided that he would live to fight again another day. He glared at Adam and then climbed up the ladder.

Adam's mind raced. Butcher was getting away with all of the items, and Ben was too far away to stop him. Besides, Ben would be too tired from the sprinting to fight. Adam decided he had to do something.

Suddenly a movie played in his mind. He remembered the box jumping when he was in the grain bin and he pulled the Impression Stone to him.

He ran back to the Radome and climbed the ladder, sticking his head up through the hole.

Inside, Butcher was standing exactly in the middle on top of the center pillar. He stood still with his hands at his sides until he noticed Adam. If looks could kill, Adam would have been lying dead on the ground, but Butcher didn't move. Rays of energy began radiating from him.

Adam remembered that Butcher had called the Radome a transporter, so he realized that he didn't have much time. He concentrated as hard as he could on the Impression Stone, then physically and mentally pulled it to him with every ounce of energy he had. The wooden box ripped through the holster and landed in Adam's hand.

In the last moment before he winked out of the Radome, Butcher noticed what Adam had done. He raised his knife to throw it, but he was too slow. He was gone before he had even lifted it all the way up.

Ben growled beneath Adam, "Get the hell out of the way kid!"

Adam looked down, "He's gone."

Ben swore and kicked the pillar, and when he had moved Adam came down.

Adam looked to where Karl lay. Gurpreet and Marius were next to him performing CPR.

Everything started moving in slow motion and Ben's voice sounded like he was talking through a steel pipe.

That's when everything went black.

He opened his eyes a while later to find he was lying in the second row of the van. Gurpreet and Marius were in the front seat talking.

"I still can't believe he's dead," said Marius, fighting back tears. "I mean, I spent so much time with him. How could I miss it that he was giving information to the enemy?"

"Don't be too hard on yourself. None of us saw it either. Even if we did, I don't think any of us wanted to believe it."

"Is he really dead," asked Adam in a drowsy voice.

Gurpreet and Marius turned to face him, the sadness heavy on their faces. They had known Karl for a long time. He was their friend and co-worker. Adam realized that it was just as difficult for them to understand as it was for himself.

Gurpreet only nodded. "I'm sorry you had to see that, and I'm sorry we didn't figure it out sooner."

"What do you mean?" asked Adam.

Gurpreet looked at Marius, then back to Adam. "Now isn't the proper time to explain. Let's get you home so you can recover properly and start this conversation at a better time. Now is a time to grieve our friend." He choked up at the word 'friend', then turned and started the van.

"What about Ben?" asked Adam.

"He's going to stay until the ambulance arrives for Karl," said Marius, his voice sounding strained.

Even though he couldn't see Karl from where he lay, Adam waved in his direction and quietly said 'goodbye' as Gurpreet drove them toward home.

CHAPTER TWENTY TWO

As soon as Adam arrived at home, Mary knew something had happened just by how terrible he looked, plus the fact that Gurpreet and Marius practically carried him into the house. She immediately demanded answers, but Gurpreet and Marius insisted Adam should go to bed while they told Mary what had happened.

From his room Adam listened as they gave her the details, as much as they knew anyway, and then asked that Adam be allowed to sleep as long as possible in the morning. They would make sure that none of Adam's friends interrupted his rest either.

When Adam heard the men leave, he pretended to be asleep when he heard his mom come up the stairs. She tapped on his door and quietly asked, "Are you asleep?"

Any other time Adam would have said nothing, but that was a night unlike any other he had ever known.

"No," he answered.

The door creaked open and Mary stuck her head inside. "Can I come in?"

Adam nodded and sat up in his bed.

"Do you want to talk about it?" she asked.

He shook his head. "They gave you most of the details."

Mary stepped over and sat down on the bed next to him. It was strange because he couldn't remember her ever doing that before.

"You really need to stop all of this almost getting killed nonsense. You're starting to remind me of your father a little too much," she giggled and then sniffled.

"Really?" asked Adam. Mary rarely talked about Ed.

"Really. That's why they made him Number 2. He was always willing to risk his own life to save someone else's."

"And you let him?"

"Well, I didn't have much choice. He was the complete opposite of Larix and all of the Decreta. They'd send a thousand men, women and children to their deaths to save any one of their own lives. Your father couldn't live with himself if he knew he could've helped but didn't. That, and he always seemed to get out of nearly hopeless situations. Sound familiar?"

Adam laughed a sad laugh. It would have been so great to know him.

After a few moments of silence, Adam brought up what was really troubling him.

"I know it shouldn't bother me so much since Karl kidnapped me and tried to sell me to Larix, but I feel so heartbroken that he's gone. I mean, I watched him die..."

Adam broke down into a full cry. "They didn't have to kill him, mom," he said through the sobs.

Mary put her arm around him and let him cry himself to sleep.

Crying it out had a strange effect on Adam. He slept better than he had in a long time. When he finally woke up at a little after 10, he felt good. The deep pit he had felt inside his chest the night before was still there, but it was much more manageable.

He dressed and climbed down the stairs, half expecting his mother to be there waiting. Instead, to his great surprise, Elianora was sitting at the table sipping a coffee.

"Good morning," she said as he stared at her.

The sight of her in his house caused a log jam of thoughts and all he could do was stand there and stare.

"Sorry to startle you, but I can assure you that I am here, sitting at your table drinking a coffee. Come sit down," she said.

As soon as she waved her hand for him to come, the log jam broke open and he was able to find his voice.

"Sorry. It's just that I was expecting my mom to be here," he said as he sat down.

"Understandable. She is at work this morning, I believe."

Adam nodded. "Yeah, I think so."

He continued to stare at her.

"How did you sleep?" she asked.

"Surprisingly well," he replied.

She nodded and smiled. "With the amount of excitement you had yesterday, I'm actually surprised you're up already."

Time ticked away during an awkward section of silence.

"You're probably wondering why I'm here," asked Elianora.

"No, actually. I'm pretty sure you want to hear my side of the story."

Elianora smiled and nodded again. "Very good. Yes, that's it actually. Do you think you are up to it yet?"

Adam thought it over. "I am so grateful that Gurpreet and Marius forced me to go straight to bed last night, because if I would have had to go over it again I would have broken down completely. This morning, though...I think I can manage."

And he began telling her the whole story from the beginning. She listened intently, nodding her head at the appropriate times, gasping at some, and generally being a great listener who doesn't interrupt the storyteller.

At the end she closed her eyes for a moment before speaking.

"First, I have to apologize to you. I am sorry we let it get too far too fast," she said, taking his hand and staring him directly in the eyes.

"What do you mean? Gurpreet said the same thing yesterday."

"What I mean is that we knew we had someone passing information to Larix and we didn't figure it out in time."

The news was a shock to Adam.

"Who is 'we'?"

"Myself, Gurpreet and Ben, of course."

"Ben?" Adam exclaimed.

Elianora nodded. "I know you've been led to believe that he isn't trustworthy, but I hope you now see you were wrong."

Adam nodded. "I'm getting there. It's just, the things he said made me think it was him. Between that and what Karl said about him..."

"Ben is one of the most loyal, decent people I know. That doesn't mean he has the slightest clue how to deal with anyone in a delicate manner. He is rough and crude, but his moral compass points north, always north. He will do anything to save anyone worth saving."

"How did he know where to find me?"

"He put a tracker on you the other night. He thought he should keep track of you. He's actually done it a couple of times. The first time was when you were fixing his lawn mower."

Adam thought about it for a moment.

"How come I didn't know about the tracker? Wouldn't I have felt it?"

Elianora shook her head. "No, not that one. It's complex, but it works with pheromones that I designed. He would just have to lightly touch you and then you could be followed for 36 hours. It doesn't give your location, but it leaves a trail that a special device can sense."

"So did Ben put a faulty spark plug in his lawn mower just to get me over and put the tracker on me?"

"Yes and no. He really did have trouble with his mower, but he knew he could fix it if he tried. He was able to confirm your ability to connect with mechanical objects and put the trace on you at the same time."

"How did he know I was missing?" asked Adam.

"Kevin came over to your house to find you, and when you weren't at your house or at Karl's he got worried. He went home and told his parents and they called Gurpreet.

As soon as Gurpreet heard that Adam was missing, he got Ben to track you down, not knowing that you were in trouble yet, but just to make sure you were ok. Ben started tracking you and when the trail led out of town, he jumped in Gurpreet's van. They picked up Marius just in case they needed another hand and they followed the trail. As they approached the farm yard, Ben thought he saw Karl's car in the distance driving away. He had a hunch that Karl was taking you to the Killaly Radome, so he had Gurpreet follow and park just out of sight while he crept in to see what was going on. Once Ben heard you yell he ran for it, and you know the rest."

"When he was talking to Butcher, he said that Butcher couldn't beat him ten years ago. They've fought before?"

Elianora nodded. "Actually, when Ben was head of security at Aeturnum, he hired Butcher. Trained him as his understudy after seeing what Butcher could do. His real name is Butch. When Ben left, Butch became head of security for a while, but then he disappeared. Aeturnum asked Ben to find Butch and make sure he was alright, but when Ben found him he discovered that Butch had gone to work for the Decreta. He barely escaped alive."

"So you knew someone was passing information," said Adam.

"We didn't know for sure, but Gurpreet suspected it. I'm the trusting old fool that said Gurpreet was just trying to find a reason that it had happened. It made sense, though. Last year, someone tipped Larix off about the Heartstone being in Grayson, and that I was here too. At the time I thought the Heartstone was still here, buried in the Radome caves. Anyway, once I had some time to think about it, I started to watch everyone to try and figure out who was the leak. I ended up letting Ben in on it because I wasn't making any headway. What we did next, I am afraid was my fault. I wanted the other

Impression Stone back anyway, so I led the senior members to believe that the Heartstone might be hidden in that statue, hoping the guilty person would call Larix and we could capture both of them trying to break into the statue. We recruited John Gunderson to help watch the statue for any unusual activity."

That woke a memory for Adam. "John was working with Karl. He's connected directly to Larix, I'm sure of it."

"John was helping *us*. What makes you think otherwise?" asked Elianora.

"Did he tell you that Karl was at the statue many times?"

"No," she replied.

"When Karl was telling me about everything he'd done, he said 'It pays to stay well connected. Knowledge is power.' That's exactly the same phrase John told me. And someone informed Karl that I had found the Impression Stone in Killaly before we even made it back to Grayson."

Elianora smiled. "That saying is one of John's favourite sayings. He's told it to me more than once before. As far as informing him about the Impression Stone, I'm not so sure. I'll have to look into it."

Adam was happy that she at least agreed to investigate John.

"So why are there two fake Heartstones and two hiding spots?" asked Adam. "Did you just have them both to throw off whoever discovered either one?"

"Yes and no," said Elianora. She picked up a familiar box that had been hiding on the floor and set it on the table. She opened the box to reveal all of the special stones.

"Remember last year when you brought me the fake Heartstone and I was surprised to learn about the Aeturnum symbol inside?"

Adam nodded.

"Well, that's because I honestly didn't know about it at the time. You see, in my arrogance, I thought that I couldn't be tortured or forced to give up any details about the location of the Heartstone. I told you that last year, remember? I was surprised by the solution Larix injected me with where I couldn't help myself. I told him everything I knew at the time, when I had assumed nothing could ever make me talk."

"I remember," said Adam.

"Something strange started happening soon after. Slowly I had a haze lift from my memories, and I realized that I've been missing a few days. In the same way, George began remembering things too, although at a slower rate than me. Remember when you joined the League and we told you that if you weren't successful at becoming a member we would wipe your memory and you wouldn't remember anything for a period of time? Well, memories are never truly gone. They are always in there somewhere," she pointed at her head. "Whatever Larix used in the gas that surrounded the town last year managed to wear away those memory blocks. Over time, I remembered that we had come up with this plan to make sure I couldn't be compromised and tell where the Heartstone really was. I blocked my own memories in the hope that it was now hiding safe for a long time. The thing is that I always like to make sure there's more than one way to uncover the location of the Heartstone. That's why I created two Impression Stones, knowing Larix couldn't read them. It's actually a really rare ability. Your dad was able to do it, and I thought Karl could too, so I was covered if I needed someone to retrieve the

Heartstone. Sadly, Karl wasn't able to connect with the Impression Stones deep enough to receive the instructions. Another thing I had overlooked."

"Karl told me that you could have given him the ability to connect deeper but wouldn't and that's why he did what he did."

Elianora shook her head. "I never thought about it at the time, but he probably heard that from Larix, or from someone on behalf of Larix. Larix probably promised to give him the ability if he betrayed us."

That's when Adam remembered the cruel message Butcher delivered right before...

He shook his head to forget that moment, and then merely nodded.

"It still doesn't explain the fakes," said Adam.

"Well, like I said, I always like to have backup plans. That's why the instructions on both Impression Stones and Heartstones were identical."

"Except for the Aeturnum symbol. You seemed surprised by that," said Adam.

Elianora nodded. "That I did not expect nor remember, even when my memory had returned. I didn't put it there when I wrote the message. I only wanted it to be a generic 'we've taken the stone' message so that Larix didn't go killing more people trying to find it. That's why I am pretty sure the Heartstone really is gone."

"If it is gone, is that going to change things around here?" he asked.

Elianora nodded.

"I know it's selfish, but I don't want things to change," he said. "I know things will anyway now that Karl's gone."

"You know, I sometimes forget just how young you are. Let me tell you something that will help you for your entire life. The only thing that will never change is the fact that change is inevitable. Do you understand that?"

"I think so..."

"It means that change will always happen, whether you want it to or not. When you are young, you only have a short window of time that you've seen, and to you, mostly, things have remained the same. I, on the other hand, am really, really old, and I see change every day. I understand how small changes snowball into large changes over time because I've seen it over and over again. If you learn to adapt to the changes around you easily, you will always be happy in your life. Do you understand?"

Adam nodded.

"Good. And don't forget that my offer still stands. If you ever need anyone to talk to, you come and see me. But that brings me to the biggest reason I am here."

Adam looked at her and instantly understood what she meant.

"You need me to try and find the Heartstone, don't you."

Elianora nodded again. "You are the one that deserves to after what you've been through, and more than that, I trust you."

Adam considered it for a moment.

"The only problem is that I still have no idea where to look."

Elianora opened the box and placed a fake Heartstone on the table along with the Grayson Impression Stone.

"Here is the answer," she said.

Adam looked at the stones then back to her.

"Sorry. Still don't get it."

"The reason we made two fake Heartstones is that if Larix managed to get hold of either one, he might find someone to read it and he would have gotten the message sending him somewhere else to look. We would still have another one, though, as a backup."

"Backup..." Adam was still confused.

"That's ok. I'm not sure you're strong enough yet, but I figured I would give you a chance."

Adam raised an eyebrow.

"You need to connect with these," said Elianora pointing at the stones on the table.

"I have already," said Adam.

"Individually, yes. Together, no."

Adam's other eyebrow raised as high as the first one before diving back down. "Really? It's that simple?"

Elianora nodded. "One Impression Stone and one Heartstone. Any combination will work."

Adam considered it for a moment before picking up the two stones. He cupped them between his hands, brought them up to his head and concentrated.

It was like the first time he had ever connected with a stone when Karl was teaching the boys how to Kurl. The connection started off a little shaky, but then he felt the familiar falling toward the center, although he was confused as to the center of what. Was it the Impression Stone, the fake Heartstone or somewhere in the middle?

After he had stopped at the center, something else came forward. What looked like a piece of paper flew forward and hung in mid-air. It was a diagram. It showed the placement of the two stones, each in a specific location. Once in place, the stones opened another door. The door was someplace he had never been, but that didn't matter. He knew exactly where it was.

CHAPTER TWENTY THREE

"Do you feel up to it?" asked Elianora.

"I think so," said Adam.

"Would it be ok if you tried this morning?" she asked.

"Sure, but I'm going to need a ride."

"It's all taken care of already," she replied as she stood.

She slipped on her shoes and stepped outside, and Adam did the same. They sauntered down the driveway until Elianora stopped. She waved at someone on the south corner of the block. It was Kevin. Kevin turned and walked out of sight behind a house, and a few moments later a large van rounded the corner.

Marius parked his vehicle right next to Adam and Elianora, and the side door opened wide. Adam's eyes showed his surprise. The van was nearly full!

Inside were Mikhail and Kevin, Gurpreet and Mark, James and Jimmy. Marius was driving and the only seat left was the passenger seat up front.

"Get in," said Mark. "I'm so squished I'm seeing stars."

"But there's no place for Elianora," said Adam.

"I can't go anyway. If the Heartstone really is there," she made the sound and motion of an explosion again.

Adam nodded.

"If it is there, Gurpreet knows what to do. Just listen to him." She handed him the box containing all of the stones.

Adam nodded again. "Thank you," he said looking her directly in the eyes.

"No – thank *you*," she replied.

Adam grinned as he turned and slid into the passenger seat.

Soon they had arrived at their destination. When Adam told Marius where they were going, his eyebrows moved between surprised and questioning looks. Having arrived with Adam telling them nothing, they all piled out of the van and stood around waiting for instructions.

The graveyard in Killaly was small just like the town, so it didn't take long for Adam to find what he was looking for. He led the group over to a grave marked by a unique headstone.

"Here lies Brutus Killaly, founder of the town that bears his name," Adam read from the plaque. He looked up at the statue above. It was an exact replica of the statue where Adam had found the Impression Stone, but only a fraction of the size.

"Don't tell me we have to dig," moaned Mark, to which everyone laughed except Gurpreet.

"I don't think so," said Adam.

He pulled the box from his pocket and opened it, taking out the Killaly Impression stone. He placed it in one hand of the statue, and then placed one of the fake Heartstones in the other hand. The moment he did, they heard a pop from somewhere behind the headstone.

Adam looked around the headstone and noticed that the grave cover immediately behind it had popped open on one side. He walked over to it and heaved it open. A staircase led down into darkness, even in the midday light.

Mark looked in and whistled. "Another mysterious cave with a completely dark stairway? Have fun down there, McTaggart."

Adam grinned. "I don't think this one's going to be as big as the one in Grayson," he said.

Gurpreet handed a small flashlight to Adam. "I always carry one of these. You should start doing that too."

Adam smiled and said 'Thanks'.

"I'll just go down by myself. That way no one else might get hurt."

"Are you sure?" asked Mike.

"I'm sure," replied Adam.

"If there's anything at all that concerns you, just yell or come back up." said Marius.

Adam stepped into the narrow staircase and slowly made his way down. As he carefully checked each step in front of him he saw the flashlight beam get shorter and shorter until he was surrounded by darkness.

"Oh man, that was just freaky!" Adam heard Mark say. "It's like your head was floating in mid air and then disappeared."

Adam smiled after hearing that, but returned to his slow descent. Quite a few steps later, he came out of the darkness and could see a small room ahead. At the end of the room was one small shelf carved into the wall, and on that shelf was a small box.

Adam took his time walking over to the box, shining the flashlight and feeling the walls next to him for a trigger, but none came. He took the box with one hand and had to hold the flashlight with his neck while he used both hands to open it up to look inside.

The only thing inside the box was a small piece of paper. On the paper was a hand-written note:

 The Heartstone safely resides at a new address. EM.

Adam recognized the handwriting immediately.

EM.

Edward McTaggart.

Dad.

ABOUT THE AUTHOR

Scott Gelowitz grew up in Grayson, Saskatchewan, and now lives in Regina, Saskatchewan, with his wife Jennifer and their four children.

Grayson is used as the main setting for this novel, and most of the places are real. The people, however, are completely fictional.

Town Secrets is the first book in the series ***The Book of Adam***.

For contact information, or information on other books in ***The Book of Adam*** series, please visit:

www.scottgelowitz.com

83861868R00150

Made in the USA
Columbia, SC
13 December 2017